Thomas C. Amory, Thomas C. (Thomas Coffin) Amory

Charles River

a poem

Thomas C. Amory, Thomas C. (Thomas Coffin) Amory

Charles River
a poem

ISBN/EAN: 9783337374099

Printed in Europe, USA, Canada, Australia, Japan

Cover: Foto ©Andreas Hilbeck / pixelio.de

More available books at **www.hansebooks.com**

A Poem.

BY

THOMAS C. AMORY,

AUTHOR OF "LIFE OF GENERAL JOHN SULLIVAN," "GOVERNOR
JAMES SULLIVAN," "SIEGE OF NEWPORT," ETC.

CAMBRIDGE:

JOHN WILSON AND SON.

University Press.

1888.

CONTENTS.

THE CHARLES RIVER.

CANTO I.

FONS.

IN ancient days, when earth and sky were young,
　The ocean breeze, from healthy vapors bred,
On crumbled rocks its humid treasures flung,
And every barren spot with verdure spread.
The summer clouds dropped down their quicken-
　　　ing showers,
The summer sunbeam all its ardor pours,
Till form and tint bedeck the turf with flowers;
Where root can cling, the tree majestic soars.
　Perchance coeval with this earliest morn
　Our stream to youth perennial was born.

Begot of dew-drops on a thousand hills,
At first a trickle, then a rill, it wells —
Its little bed of sand and pebbles fills;
At every turn its tiny volume swells;

Mid flag and moss now timid shrinks from view,
Then bolder leaps in joy from ledge to ledge,
Smiles back to heaven its more celestial blue,
Till, tired of play, it hides amidst the sedge,
  Demurely gliding on, a purling brook,
  To find a cradle in some shady nook.

Beneath the arching boughs, in sylvan glade,
Brimming the bowl the barring rocks provide,
Its gathering waters burst in bold cascade,
Or, murmuring down the dell, in music glide.
The insect's hum, the melancholy loon,
The early buds perfuming all the air,
The fleecy clouds that veil the crescent moon,
The rustling leaves, the cooing mates that pair,
  The guardian stars that pierce the covert high,
  All soothe to sleep, — kind Nature's lullaby.

But when again the flush of early dawn
Flooded with purple light the brightening east,
From out the sea the ruddy disk of morn
Aroused from nest and cave each bird and beast;
Its golden beams illuming first the west,
Then streamed effulgent through primeval wood,
The long-drawn aisles in brilliant lustre drest,
Each lofty trunk in radiant splendor stood;

And with the placid pool that slumbers there
The vaulted arches all their glories share.

From pleasant dreams the sleeping stream awoke,
To view with glad surprise th' enchantment round;
From off his limbs the drowsy fetters shook,
From off his soul, refreshed, the spell that bound.
A grateful sense that powers above, divine,
This ever-varying loveliness create,
Transforms th' illumined groves to fane and shrine;
For no vain hecatombs to chance or fate,
   But fitting altar to the living God
   Amid the gardens that His steps have trod.

And many birds, of various plumage, sing,
Or, hovering round the mossy brink, alight
And in its crystal waters dip the wing,
Bask in the sun and then resume their flight.
From branch to branch the squirrels leap in play,
Or mock the coilèd snake that tempts beneath;
The fox, as crafty, lies in wait for prey
That find no terrors in their destined death,
   Since so ordained that all allowed to live,
   The food they take must be content to give.

The morning rays ruddied the jutting crag
Where, canopied in leaves, there stood agaze,

Screened partially from view, a stately stag,
Scanning the fairy scene with pleased amaze;
Yet with instinctive caution, lest some foe
May lurk within the thicket, his keen eye
Marks every quivering branch above, below,
T' avoid the peril that he cannot fly;
    Assured at last no danger menaced, then
    With silent steps he ventured up the glen.

Instinct, but reason in a less degree,
To structure, purpose, circumstance, conforms;
Spiders their web, its hive constructs the bee,
The lazy bear sleeps through the winter's storms;
What constitutes its kind is found in each,
Throughout the centuries it changes not;
Should some new clime another habit teach,
The like good sense attends their altered lot:
    Completeness thus designed proves Providence,
    Not gradual evolution out of chance.

The nimble deer leaps gayly through the snow,
Or basks content beneath the summer's noon;
The birds, that all the varying seasons know,
Pursue what suits them best from zone to zone;
And where, for each, mature their favorite plants,
Flock after flock swoop down with weary wing.

Salmon for ocean depths forsake their haunts, —
The brawling stream they frolicked up in spring;
  Yet when another's warmth its limbs unbind,
  Their natal river never fail to find.

Once on the stream, before the trapper's tread
The solemn stillness of its woods disturbed,
By natural law or heavenly guidance led,
The beaver tribes, each selfish impulse curbed.
Felled down the loftiest trees to dam their pond,
Constructed houses no one dared molest;
Each of his mate considerate and fond,
Each his own task at labor, with the rest.
  If Providence in them such sense implant,
  Why not in us, to share with bee and ant?

Hid mid the trees and rocks with lichens draped,
In some still pool or deep unrippled run,
The furtive trout, the angler's snare escaped,
Darts at the flies that hover in the sun;
At times, deluded by the tempting bait,
By hook concealed, the fish himself is caught, —
The more he struggles with his hapless fate,
The surer victim of the craft, he taught;
  So often we are called upon to bear
  The woe that we for other men prepare.

No more the beast of prey these vales molests;
No reptiles venomous in covert lurk;
The hawk and eagle elsewhere build their nests,
And time obliterates the beaver's work;
No anglers here can longer tempt the trout,
No greedy pickerel leap to take the hook;
The sportsman vaunts his dogs he ne'er takes out,
And reads of woodcock, partridge, in his book.
  The region once abounded in its game, —
  All gone, though many a stream still bears the
    name.

As ages pass, progressive silence sheds
New lustre on the purposes of God;
His glorious earth in ampler beauty spreads
With richer forests and more verdant sod;
The hills and streams with fuller courses flow,
And ponds and lakes reflect His living light;
The wingèd fowls fresh germs of fragrance strow;
The quickening beams, the grateful dews of night,
  The changing seasons, with their unchanged laws,
  Obey His will, of all the first great cause.

The work completed, as fit homes for man
How matters not, men hither come to dwell,
Finding throughout the universal plan

Proof of their title needs no tongue to tell.
Well may it be that from some elder realm
The winds and waves them wafted from the shore,
Glad to escape the billows that o'erwhelm,
And little tempt to brave their billows more;
Each want supplied, they care no longer roam,
Accept with grateful hearts their destined home.

Much as in times remote, it is to-day;
The rocks and forest, every pond and fen;
Our stream, the Quineboquin, works its way
Among the hills and through the tangled glen;
Growing in volume as its water-shed
Embraced, expanding, all the regions round,
Its quicker currents ploughed a deeper bed,
Till in the open sea repose it found;
To those hate priestly rule or regal powers,
Open the gates to this bright land of ours.

In gurgling music, through the thickets run
The frolic brooks, on dew and snow-flake fed;
The lakelets smiling, kissing in the sun,
Light all around the boundless water-shed;
From out their margins soar the woods aloft,
Repeat, reversed, their images below;
The slopes swell up with cloudy shadows soft,

Quickening the currents in their downward flow;
  Thus, intermingling, from the sky and hill
  The water-drops the ponds and rivers fill.

What special source be deemed the fountain's head
Of Quineboquin, not for us to tell;
Over this broad expanse of country spread,
Innumerable the springs that gush and well;
Not voiceless Echo, with its limpid flow
From Hopkinton, once Frankland's paradise,
Upon whose ripples lately ours to row,
Where simple joys for simple hearts suffice;
  As Charles at Milford all too lusty grown
  For Echo Lake to be its source alone.

Here a cathedral of the living God,
The leaf-clothed ledges for its nave and aisle,
Amidst the gardens that His feet have trod, —
His will creative reared this sacred pile;
Its clustering columns, with their capitals,
Circle the azure dome unflecked by cloud;
While summer tints with gold its pictured walls,
The winter spreads around its maiden shroud,
  And glorious voices of the storms of time
  Pour forth the anthems of their joy sublime.

What fitter cradle for creation's shrine,
Bosomed aloft in the eternal hills,
Soaring majestic with a grace divine,
From forest, all the slopes and valleys fills.
In the embraces of maternal arms
The infant Charles here frolics into birth;
Enwrapping sunbeams its pure spirit warms,
Lapped in the moisture of the oozing earth;
  And hovering angels hymn its lullaby,
  No sign or sound of human being nigh, —

Save where some sill decayed, or broken wall
Of perished cot or ancient farm-house rude,
The checkered memory of the dead recall
Once woke the echoes of this solitude, —
Save one old barn that from the meadow rears
Its gray decrepitude above the rock,
Long since abandoned by the kine and steer,
By bleating sheep or by the morning cocks ;
  Its lofts capacious may whole harvests hold,
  Reaped from these marshes that the Charles
    enfold.

Of grain no more for early flail to thresh,
No more the plough disturbs the humid ground
That August noon, with breezes cool and fresh,

We gazed enchanted on the scene around;
Late copious showers, freshening turf and tree,
Gleamed in that cloudless sun from frequent pool,
And sparkling rivulets in merry glee
Rushed wildly on like happy lads from school,
 Gayly unconscious of their destined lot
  To merge in brother streams and be forgot.

Yet in that amphitheatre of hills
Enclosed this spacious vale, their early home,
Enough for them the joy the moment fills,
Nor know nor care what with the future come;
Their crystal drops may not as yet reflect
The strange vicissitudes await their course
As they speed on, the sky and earth connect,
Or in the boundless waves to lose their force;
 Till, reabsorbed, some pitying cloud may wing
  Their pearls of dew back to their natal spring.

Our tireless steed tied to the rustic gate,
Perhaps the dam of many a well-bred foal,
Upon a log near by we, resting, sate,
While my companion hearkened to my scroll;
Long had my heart been busy with my theme,
And, oft in doubt, still to conviction clung
That what our charter told us were no dream,

But this the fountain whence our river sprung;
  And where on earth more fittingly than here
  Historic stream begin its proud career?

We rose refreshed, to take one lingering glance
Of all the silent splendors of the place;
Then, lest some mystic influence entrance,
Haste down the dale with ever quickening pace.
Straight as an arrow speeding from the bow
The broadening stream pursues its onward way;
Through meads luxuriant its waters flow,
While all the folding heights their tribute pay;
  Though different names for miles these stream-
      lets bore,
  Soon all to merge, to part for nevermore.

Uncas, what mingled traits of guile and pride
Lift their dark phantoms as we pass thy lake,
Or on its breast in graceful shallop glide,
Against its sylvan cliffs the echoes wake;
Untutored statesmen of a distant age,
In simple wisdom rival of the best,
None that, more valiant, deadly warfare wage
To keep the realm their hero sires possessed;
  Choosing to perish by the red man slain,
  Than foes they hated with such proud disdain.

CANTO II.

WAMPANOAGS.

AND who can say how long the time since first
    Man, as its monarch, ruled this forest land,
And weaker creatures, as they slaked their thirst,
Fell helpless victims to his ruthless hand?
When fitted to become his dwelling-place,
The wolf and hawk slew each its daily food;
Why not created all these beasts of chase
By kind intent for his especial good?
    Why, without fields to till or stock to tend,
    Should he reject what Providence may send?

His food and raiment, by creation's plan,
He took, where found, by cunning, force, or skill;
Did he provoke to war his fellow-man?
No conscience whispered that he should not kill.
Safety consisted in his being strong;
Nor only so, but that his foes beware;
To stigmatize as savage does him wrong, —
To guard against destruction his sole care.

Not for himself alone, but child and wife,
For whom each day he fearless risked his life.

They kept no records; no traditions tell
The source from whence their dusky race proceeds;
Complete were the conditions where they dwell,
Or by degrees evolved to meet their needs;
Such as they were when first by history known,
They are to-day, substantially the same;
In form and coloring all their traits their own,
Unchanged the huntsman, as unchanged his game.
    Vices the white man brought have left their
        trace;
    No changed condition modifies the race.

From shore to shore, from tropic to the pole,
Their tribes for ages self-controlled remained;
One faith, one law and custom for the whole,
Each its own separate water-shed retained;
Their names so musical revealed their sense
Of the poetic both to sight and mind,
And loftiest sentiments their eloquence,
With fervor, strength, and tenderness combined.
    The evil in the world by spells withstood,
    The God they worshipped was both great and
        good.

Close by that sea whose daily whispers tell
Whatever chances over all the world,
The Indian knew but little that befell
His nearest neighbor, from whose wigwam curled
The smoke, to prove that other men exist,
Yet gave no intimation far away;
Nations in turn, emerging from the mist
Of time, by feats of valor fought their way
    To empire, till, by fortune spoiled, their pride
    Left them a wreck; their slaves, set free, deride.

We judge him harshly, not by what he was
Before degraded by our selfish creed,
When guided simply by protective laws
He followed where his inborn instincts lead;
The royal guest of Champlain's festal hall,
Castines, whose blood flows with the best of France,
Were Nature's noblemen, endowed with all
The traits that neither rank nor birth enhance;
    Modest and faithful, loyal, brave, and just,
    As Sydney, Bayard, or the noblest dust.

What cordial welcome that of Samoset!
What host more bountiful than Ivanhoe?
No saintlier soul than Hobomok's as yet
Stood ever faster friend in weal or woe;

The princely Chikatawbut, sagamore
Of all the forest realm our river feeds,
Broad Mystic's queen, the gracious sachem squaw,
Our sure reliance in our direst needs,
  Though oft by base ingratitude provoked,
  Begrudged no friendly services invoked.

Narrow, contentious, with no grateful sense
Of blessing, — conceiving that God creates
All for saints elect, and hath no Providence
For such as enter not the special gates;
The earth their own, if Indian seek to stay
Greed that would drive him to the wood and
     hills;
Theirs to command, as his but to obey, —
What marvel that the red man scalps and kills;
  That Massasoit's sons, with knife and smoke,
  Throw off the bonds these saintly miscreants
     broke?

The noble Wampas, in his simple trust,
Had sold for scanty pay the springs of Charles;
His broad inheritance, for worthless dust
Or idle promise, by these treacherous carles
Justice denied, he sought the monarch's throne;
The King bade Leverett see the wrong redressed.

Leverett was honest, but he stood alone, —
The pious robbers still the land possessed.
　The indignant sachems saw no hope remained;
　Not to resent such wrong their honor stained.

They learned our language better than we theirs,
They practised the religion that we taught,
Gave land and corn and game in equal shares,
Against our Pequot foes their warriors fought;
But when, at last, perceived the fixed design
For all this trust and kindness but to sweep
Their race from lands their own by right divine,
They rose in might, their just revenge to steep
　In the base blood that such requital gave
　For all their generous deeds to help and save.

The Wampanoags, when Massasoit reigned
And friendly welcome to the invaders gave,
All the broad realm which bears his name retained,
From the high mountain to the ocean wave;
The Nipmuck chiefs, his vassal lords, bore sway
Where Merrimack leads down her tribute streams;
And other tribes along the Nashua,
Whose rapid tide with noble salmon teems,
　And brave Canonchat, Narragansett's lord,
　King Philip's lead accept with one accord.

For twelve long weary months the war they waged
Where now three million souls contented dwell;
Two rival races, pitiless, enraged,
Savage and brutal, as if fiends of hell,
Contended for the privilege of life;
Each seeking to annihilate its foe,
Retaliations but envenomed strife,
Each dastard act but striking back its blow:
   The issue trembled in a doubtful scale,
   Which, forest king or stranger, should prevail.

Not far from where the river flows its course,
Its current ran with blood from hostile veins;
The tomahawk was plied without remorse,
The scalping-knife the blood of woman stains;
Where Medway, Medfield, bound upon its stream,
May yet be traced th' intrenchments round the fort
The settlers built; in case their nightly dream
Became reality, they might transport
   Their wives and children, and what else they prize
   Might there be brought, secure against surprise.

Five hundred warriors, by King Philip led,
Drew near, the winter's night, the place forlorn;
With stealthy steps the forest paths they tread,
No guard, no watch-dog, on th' alert to warn;

Each brave in silence at his post stood still,
When signal given, each settler's house ablaze,
They slew and spared not while remained to kill,
Yet oft delayed to torture, till they craze;
    Nor age, nor sex, nor infant helplessness
    Escape the fury that these fiends possess.

The flames by night, the cloud of smoke by day,
Arouse the people all the country round
To reinforce the fort; in brave array
They man the parapet, the tocsin sound;
Th' alarum spreads the startling call to arms;
In gath'ring strength, with bolder hearts, they come;
The smould'ring ruins, devastated farms,
Remind each soldier he too has a home;
    A council held, their several leaders choose,
    And to prepare for fight no moment lose.

Nor had they long to wait. In serried rank,
Each nation by itself, from out the wood
Emerged to seek some unprotected flank,
Where their fierce onset could be least withstood.
No such weak point the strong defences show,
Veterans in war, their plan without reproach;
The leafless trees, the lake of frozen snow,
Exposes all around the near approach.

King Philip sees his only chance depends
Upon the strength superior valor lends.

Upon his numbers, too; his force, they say,
In that exceeded what stood by the fort.
He marshalled well his men to work their way
With slow advances, by experience taught,
Behind the walls and covers, till they reach
A point of vantage whence their guns will tell,
And seize the moment that the chance may teach
For desperate onslaught, with their wonted yell;
Philip himself, his men to form and lead,
Rode fearless, midst the fire, his coal-black steed.

From many a rifle, spoil of fallen foe,
The well-aimed bullets of the Indians sped;
Both sides lost heavily, yet no tremor show
As brave and true men, where they stood, fell
        dead;
Amidst the smoke, beneath its sable shroud,
The Indians, yelling, rush across the field,
When booming cannon on the mangled crowd
Belch forth their horrors, from their ports concealed;
    The staggered throng, mowed down, at last retreat,
    Trampling their dying comrades 'neath their
        feet.

Two hundred warriors slain, their chieftains sought
Those left to rally for renewed attack;
But seen the havoc that the cannon wrought,
In sullen sadness led their forces back.
Burning the bridge, and laden with their spoil,
They gained a hill remote, for rest and food;
They mourned their dead; then, weary with their
    toil,
Sought refuge under shelter of the wood;
  With varying fortune they prolonged the strife,
  Ending, ere long, with their great chieftain's life.

And now, with Philip dead, no hope remained;
Too proud the mercy they denied, to crave,
No coward fear their last sad moment stained,
They welcomed death and the untimely grave;
One bitter thought their parting souls appalled,
Winging their way from hunting-grounds below,
That they must leave their conquered race en-
    thralled,
And cruel task-masters no pity show;
  Still, huntsmen, well they knew superior might
  In strife with weakness ever makes the right.

As little changed as Indian or his game,
The Charles flows on in the same channels now

As centuries before the white man came,
Down the long valley from the mountain's brow;
From slope and lake the sister streamlets rush,
Fondly in one the numerous waters blend;
From all their secret springs the currents gush,
The dew of morn, the winter's tempest, lend
    Such equal measure, as to rarely shrink,
    Or in excess to overflow its brink.

CANTO III.

MOUNT PEGAN.

HOW near akin the river's course and time
    Our human life, for each of us, for all;
Its fountains, mid the snowy peaks sublime,
Creep innocently on or heedless fall;
Its frolic play, youth's fevered, fervid glow,
Our manhood's prime of generous thought and
      deed,
Unvalued laurels for the wrinkled brow,
The heaped-up riches that survive the greed;
    And when at last all that we hoped to be,
    Swept on, resistless, to the hungry sea.

Latest and noblest on creation's scale,
What now or may be, embryo in the germ,
His wondrous capabilities avail
No more for man than in the lowliest worm,
Unless occasion, circumstance, conspire
With education and ambitious spur

To kindle in his soul its latent fire,
And wisdom, temper, character, concur,
    Not in the silent solitary man,
    But on society's well-ordered plan.

Reason, speech, conscience, and a vivid sense
Of souls immortal, of harmonious laws
That govern mind and matter, the immense
Of spiritual being, up to their great Cause
Who shapes and guides the universal plan,
With capabilities that constitute
Our life a priceless privilege, raises man,
Made in God's image, far above the brute;
    If less than angel, and too prone to stray,
    Not His the fault who shows the better way.

Though such the possibilities conferred
On each of us, and all of human kind,
The favored few, and on the common herd
Corporeal function, faculty of mind;
Though ages in their course have wrought no
       change,
Each race, as earliest known, the same to-day, —
There still are limitations, and the range
In European greater than Malay;
    Yet in each race the differences are,
    Between its best and vilest, wider far.

Beats there a heart that does not faster throb
At noble deed or maiden loveliness,
The pictured charms that art from Nature robs,
Or Nature's own, that Deity express?
Who can, as sets the sun, unmoved behold
The parting beams light up the boundless scene,
Of purpled russet or of limpid gold,
The shifting shades that float in misty sheen,
    Or autumn coloring, chastened and subdued,
    Not to disturb that quiet solitude?

With soul at ease, in autumn's golden haze
Climb Pegan's heights, and from amidst the glow
Look down in silent awe with raptured gaze
Upon the varied beauty spread below.
There sweeps the river with majestic grace,
Its waters flushing with declining day;
Now circling with its arms the mountain's base,
Then speeding rapidly in foam away
    By the stone shaft in Eliot's honor wrought,
    Who living waters to the Indians brought.

Another monument, that sacred tome,
Made plain his message in their native tongue;
His only care to bring the wanderers home,
With them he prayed, with them in fervor sung;

He knows no rest, no peril could dismay
His soul devoted to the cross he bore;
No thirst for praise his spirit led astray:
Let them accept the faith, he asked no more.
   Here, where he gathered in his dusky fold,
   Such right as his to sainthood may be told.

The simple precepts that the Gospels teach,
The saint, the child, the savage understand;
The various dogmas which the churches preach
May serve as landmarks in a dreary land;
Questions that Indian acolytes propound,
Displaying oft acute intelligence,
Minds more enlightened than their own confound
By native wit and merest common-sense;
   Their answers keen, as sword the Gordian knot,
   Solve many a problem that the sage cannot.

When Father Gabriel sat by Eliot's hearth, —
Two saints, one Roman and one Puritan,
Who each had traversed many a weary path
To teach the Indian what Christ taught to man, —
Though far apart their creed and rite may be,
And not forgot their heritage of hate,
Not where they differ, but in what agree,
Is borne in mind as they their toils relate.

In hearts like theirs no hostile feelings lurk
As they take counsel for their blessed work.

It was the Christmas-tide; Quebec was far,
And dangers numberless beset the way, —
The winter snows and seas, and Indian war, —
In vain the pastor urged his guest to stay;
But when the spring more genial season brought,
They visited Nonantum, " place of hills; "
Together there the forest children taught,
Where Nature's sanctity its temple fills.
  Sure, since our Saviour's sermon on the mount
  None more like that can chronicles recount.

Not all their preaching vain, for many a heart
Did truly learn by practice what they taught,
If others not.   It may be that in part
Christian professions often came to naught;
Tho' Puritans read much the Book inspired,
Their greed insatiate and their temper stern,
The lands they coveted, by force acquired,
For service rendered made but poor return.
  If Christians would the soul of Pagan reach,
  They must more truly practise what they preach.

If not all equal, while with steadfast trust
We hear, at gates above, the herald's call,

How can we doubt the Infinite is just,
Though earthly scales poise not alike for all?
The faith that Eliot taught, the crucifix,
Had little strange for braves from childhood trained
To bear unflinching all that pain inflicts, —
Their ruling motive, pride, alone had changed.
 Sprinkled with waters dashing pure and free,
 They bore their cross in proud humility.

But standing here upon this sacred hill,
With Wauban's blushing waters not remote,
How can we doubt that other saints may still,
Like Eliot, strive to follow what he wrote?
The cloistered walls that lift above the trees
Their battlements, to shield from ignorance,
May send forth multitudes to guide or please,
To leave examples noble as Durant's.
 Nor will that love which fills the earth with
  flowers
 Go unremembered in this world of ours.

But nearer still extends for many a rood
An Eden of delight for every age,
Gardens and lawns, the pond and stream and
  wood,
Whatever else may idle hours engage.
The spacious halls that teem with happy life,

Each summer's tide, enchanted castle prove.
The childish games of rivalry and strife
Grow year by year to more abiding love;
 And through their sorrows many a wedded pair
 Find solace in the vows they plighted there.

Who is there but remembers this fair world
Has other beauties than what meets the eye:
That every wreath of smoke from house-top curled,
Denotes the abode of each domestic tie
That makes of our existence weal or woe?
If cursed, then death has little more to dread;
If blessed, then Heaven can little more bestow;
Yet where by faith each mortal spirit led,
 The years may flit, and youth old age become,
 Without a wish that ours another home.

Along the banks in mouldering beauty stand
Abodes, the earliest of their fathers reared;
Comely and quaint, if spacious not nor grand,
By sacred memories to their hearts endeared;
If kindred groups no Yule or Easter brought,
About the ample hearth, from homes remote,
Thanksgiving came with equal promise fraught, —
The farmers prize their kin of greater note;
 Beneath the roof with grasp fraternal greet:
 Who parted youths, in manly vigor meet.

Ranged on the settles, round the blazing logs,
The aged grandam, smiling in her joy,
Forgets how time her own warm pulses clogs,
As she again beholds each girl and boy;
And in her children marks familiar trace
Of those long mounted to the realms above;
That angel look or that remembered grace
Long years efface not from maternal love;
    The course of time accepts without dismay,
    Since those thus dearly cherished lead the way.

Yet not alike for all.   The stream divides
Two regions; one with frequent dwellings set,
With crowded villages, rich farms, besides
Whatever thrift and industry beget;
The frequent church denotes their souls devout,
And schools the value they in knowledge place;
And mills and workshops scattered all about
Bespeak a vigorous, energetic race;
    With wholesome tasks for each who cares to earn,
    For all whose hearts for nobler objects burn.

Off to the east and south, upon the right,
Where scarce a hundred homes now dot the waste,
Continuous woods, where Philip fought his fight,
For miles and miles the varied surface graced;

The oaks and ashes, hemlock and the pine,
Had there for ages stood in grand array;
Kings of the forest by a right divine,
They held their solemn conclave day by day;
    And when the winds grew chill, and summer gone,
    Kept festival, with all their bravery on.

There ranged the deer, and there in covert lone
The fretted stag his branching antlers shed;
The lofty moose, for generations gone,
Stalked through the moonlit glades with stately
    tread;
Trout filled the brooks, and passing snipe would
    stray
From off the shore to fatten on their brink;
The prowling wolf and panther kept away,
Or cautiously approached their banks for drink;
    The mouldering trees, upheaved by winter's
    storms,
    Leant weird against the rest their spectral forms.

But when the settlers came, the woodman's axe
Cut off what growth their careless brush-fires spare;
The sterile soil all warmth and vigor lacks,
The plains remained untilled, the hillsides bare;
Without the shade, the rains to vapor turn,

The streams, once brimming, shrink to useless rills;
The summer sunbeams all the grasses burn;
No flocks or herds can live upon the hills.
  This fearful warning, told and told again,
  Should rouse from lethargy all thoughtful men.

That Love divine that crowds the universe
With sentient life, for happiness and growth,
By blessings tempts our human kind, perverse,
To think and work, — by want dissuades from
      sloth;
To reap rich harvests from a fertile soil
Develops all our faculties and powers,
To plough and sow and weed with watchful toil,
To irrigate when fail the needed showers;
  Yet too much moisture, with its vapors dank,
  Breeds bog or fen or vegetation rank.

All round the earth sad instances are found
Of lands, once fertile, useless and untilled,
The sheltering shade removed from off the ground,
The soil let loose, the river courses filled;
The people poor, illiterate, enslaved,
The nation powerless against its foe,
The rule despotic, and its chiefs depraved,
And all because the rivers cease to flow;

Because a senseless greed neglects to plant
Forests, the coming times will sadly want.

With turn abrupt reversing then its course,
The stream sweeps by in front of where we gaze,
Then like an arrow with abating force,
With the last parting beams its breast ablaze,
It coils along, a dozen miles or more,
By Needham's plains or Dover's forests dense,
Its tributary streamlets by the score
With lushest growth mantling the vast expanse;
The splendor of its autumn tints subdued
As night comes down upon the solitude.

CANTO IV.

MOTHER BROOK.

MOMENTS seem hours as we lingering dwell,
　　Yet shadows deepen, and the loftier spires
In white array send back their last farewell
As sinks the orb, and parting day expires, —
Yet not to instant darkness leaves the scene;
Around its couch a bright effulgence pours;
The clouds above, opposing hills between,
Far up the skies the tinted radiance soars,
　　And shapes suggestive that forever change
　　Heap up in graceful forms their semblance
　　　　strange.

That side the sinking sun with glory fills
A flood of many waters from the lakes,
Mount Nebo is, with brotherhood of hills;
Through wooded dales its course the river takes,
By Natick, once the praying Indian's home,
By graves wherein their generations sleep,

3

Where many a worthy patriarch still has come
His watch against the judgment day to keep;
   Then rushes on to gather in the flow
   From Wauban, spreading wide in sunset glow.

The last faint flush fades slowly from the sky,
Some one lone star emits its opal light,
Another and another gleams on high;
And now the myriad lustres of the night,
Orion and the Pleiad and the Wain,
The clustered galaxies or distant sun,
Which each successive eve return again,
Our sister orbs that nearer courses run, —
   All shed their glories on the placid stream,
   Which, wrapt in their effulgence, floats a dream.

The nearest often seems the brightest star:
Thine, Motley, neither space nor time can dim;
More highly prized, perchance, in lands afar,
Here fortune filled thy goblet to the brim;
If midst its dregs some Marah drop, concealed,
Imbittered to the taste its latest draught,
Too versed in all that history revealed
To doubt what oft is with least pleasure quaffed,
   May prove more wholesome to the parting soul
   Than the more luscious flavors of the bowl.

Much we may mourn that power should be unjust,
Yet its injustice cannot worth debase;
Time works its vindications, and our trust
In honest pens like thine we safely place;
Research profound, and truth that cannot swerve,
To attract attention or indulge caprice,
Which blames or praises with discreet reserve
By honor guarded against prejudice;
 Events re-happen on thy living page,
 The historic dead again resume the stage.

An honored scion of our common race,
Symmetrical alike in form and mind,
In social intercourse an inborn grace,
Courteous and genial, gentle, frank, and kind;
Bold for the right, intolerant of wrong,
Wit, quick and keen, that flashed but never seared,
With temper ardent and a purpose strong,
With generous traits that all he knew endeared,
 A voice attuned to all he felt or said,
 His friends still heard it as his page they read.

That voice is still familiar; that large room on
  high,
With its roc's egg and marvels from the sea,
Whose little windows front the western sky, —

There oft his playmates gathered in their glee;
Later, at school away, we built our hut
In Crony Village, where a score beside
Along the valley ranged; and, portals shut,
In mirthful talk the hours of winter glide,
  While apples roast, and toasting chestnuts burst,
  And cider of our making slaked the thirst.

We skate by moonlight where the tanner's pile
In grand proportions stretches to the stars,
Gallop through forest paths for many a mile,
Or tramp for days until our wounds are scars;
We fence, swim, dance, with each his garden lot,
Climb ropes, pitch quoits, or cast the iron bar;
Speak half-a-dozen tongues, and many a knot
Of science solve in disputatious war;
  And laurels blooming over many a field
  Presage, for one like him, of honor yield.

Nor was the presage vain.   In college walls
His brilliancy and various scholarship,
In club, the press, or legislative halls
His racy eloquence of pen and lip
Gave him repute; while tales of local lore
Proved harbinger of works which brought renown,
And taught the nations how, for evermore,

T' escape the thraldom of both church and crown;
Twice called abroad to represent our own,
He was as greatly loved as widely known.

Midst all the strange vicissitudes of life,
Higher or lowlier, the love of home,
Some refuge from anxiety and strife
We call our own, however far we roam,
Becomes an instinct; and our fond desire
Is to transmit, in our own name and race,
Whatever we inherit or acquire,
That it may still remain the dwelling-place
Of all our generations; but this may not,
Where all are equal, often be the lot.

Here, where at Riverdale he came to dwell,
The river circled it with fond embrace,
Ling'ring as if 't were loath to break the spell
That bound its sluggish currents to the place;
Close by Brook Farm, the sage's paradise,
Orchards whose juices with Champagne's com-
pare,
A smiling lake in the near foreground lies, —
Beyond, the Massasoit's summits bare;
Around their base the dark Neponset glides,
Collecting tribute from their craggy sides.

For ride or stroll, or for the sportsman's quest,
Few spots can any such enticements boast;
Its rural scenes of every charm possessed, —
The forest dense, its deep-indented coast,
An infinite variety of lakes;
Massa and Punkapog, with Indian name —
The self-same view to-day the wanderer takes,
From Strawberry Banks, that to the death-bed
    came
  Of exiled Hutchinson, whose heart it broke
  No longer on that scene he loved, to look.

Due east beyond the hills not far away
Gorges at Weymouth settled on the shore ;
Going home to die, his followers would not stay, —
Some crossed the ocean to return no more.
Blackstone for years in peaceful solitude
His orchards planted and his roses culled;
He read his books in contemplative mood,
Or up the Charles for fish or beaver sculled;
  With none to trouble, none his course to scan,
  He dwelt near by its mouth, a happy man.

Morton, more social, with his jovial crew
On Merry Mount his wicked May-pole raised;
Their fun and revelry to riot grew,

Till Plymouth's Pilgrim saints pronounced them
      crazed;
Led by Miles Standish conquered them in fight,
Burnt down their May-pole and their festal hall,
And shipped their prisoners off in sorry plight, —
For mirth they deemed most heinous sin of all.
    Out of the hermit's cot and Morton's dance
    Motley's fresh genius wove his best romance.

Not far remote his brother's stately hall,
Wide-spreading parks, with sylvan treasures rare,
Bequeathed for public purposes, that all
In Nature's pure and noblest joys may share;
A sire, of social circles the delight,
Of manly vigor, generous, just, and good,
Mother whose grace and dignity unite
All that can charm in peerless womanhood, —
    With such a home, and such a lot to bless,
    What could the least contented more possess?

Motley could not be idle, and his fame
High on the roll of authorship is found;
His cherished home stands in a stranger's name,
Still, that he dwelt there sanctifies the ground;
Near by its gate a mouldering mansion stands,
Has passed for seven descents from sire to son,

Upon its spacious hearth still burn the brands,
Along the walls extends the patriarch's gun;
    Its long, sloped roof the mossy lichens stained;
    Its rooms for twelve score years remained un-
        changed.

The changing seasons, as the year revolves,
May swell the streams or shrink them in their
        beds;
When autumn fills their springs, or snow dissolves,
The overflow along the meadows spreads;
Charles and Neponset, here two miles apart,
On either side of ancient Dedham flow,
As later, thrice of Boston's busy mart;
And when united, where the ground lies low,
    Canoes for forty miles can work their way
    Between their several outlets in the bay.

And all around in mystic whispers tell
Of legends strange, of patriot, sage, and saint, —
Quincys who still in honored affluence dwell
On lands their own since the first settlement;
Their history with their country's interwove,
As their distinguished sires seven centuries since,
Who loyal to the cause of freedom prove,
As knights of yore were faithful to their prince.

Their earliest home is tilled by stranger hands,
The mansion still in stately beauty stands.

Born in the neighboring manse, within its door
Th' illustrious Hancock wooed and won his bride;
Their marriage bells the tocsin of the war
Which wrenched our freedom from a monarch's
      pride;
With all to hope if he obeisance made
To that stern tyrant's arbitrary power,
He loved his country and her call obeyed,
Her staff and light to cheer her darkest hour;
    The first to pledge his honor, wealth, and life
    To bring her scathless through the pending
      strife.

If not in genius first, or eloquence
To guide, persuade, and fire the nation's heart,
His genial nature, practical good-sense,
And general readiness to bear his part
Supplied resources, shattered ranks renewed,
Inspired with confidence; when lost, restored;
Furnished the powder and procured the food;
When timid wavered, drew himself the sword:
    A willing martyr at his country's call,
    Upon the scaffold or the field to fall.

And was his country grateful?   Some were not,
And homage paid to men who less deserved,
His noble lead in trying times forgot,
His open purse, which oft the cause preserved;
Yet while he lived, save when the Federal head,
The highest office his within the State;
Nor were there many who the struggle led
In worth and deed than him more truly great;
   Pardon to Adams and himself denied, —
   Both equally their rescued country's pride.

Yet neither rank, nor power, nor monument,
Without desert, oft earn the world's applause;
The patriot, martyr, statesman eloquent,
Who shapes the policy, improves the laws,
Rescues from peril, leads in all the ways
That make the people happy, wise, and good,
Who never intrigues, envies, or betrays, —
Such well deserve their country's gratitude;
   Our history records a glorious throng
   Whose names and fame to every age belong.

In yonder church, in honored dust, repose
Two more that bore their fellow-martyr's name, —
Father and son, whose cherished memory glows
Among the foremost in the shrines of fame;

Their long careers, in loftiest stations spent,
Embraced, together, near a century's span;
Each in his prime the nation's President, —
What higher honor is conferred on man?
   And in whatever sphere of duty placed,
   Their fitness for its claims the office graced.

CANTO V.

NEWTON.

THIS world combines, unmarred by human greed,
    All beauty that can charm or grandeur awe;
Decay itself but the life-giving seed
Of fresh enchantment to what pleased before:
The boundless woods, of every tint and kind,
Ocean in storm and calm, in lights and shades,
The mighty rivers, and the brook that winds
Its crystal music through the glens and glades;
    And hoary mountains, with their crests sublime,
    By tempests torn, the monuments of time.

What soul devout but sees in Nature's plan
God's loving heart throughout His works ex-
      pressed, —
Care for the lowliest creature as for man;
Providing not alone for food and rest,
But all that renders life a priceless boon,
Of occupations to beguile, delight,

A ceaseless round to every taste attune,
Of needs, affections, which the whole unite
   In one vast happy world of tempered joy,
   And simple pleasures which can never cloy?

On wealth or want no greater ill can fall
Than what may chance for both, — indifference
To blessings manifest, vouchsafed to all
With faithful hearts and fair intelligence:
The flowers and birds, the seasons as they change,
The vernal growth, and winter's mantle spread;
Along the stream or up the hills to range,
And fond affections sure as daily bread;
   Grateful for blessings Providence may lend,
   Content though trials Providence may send.

Could all the watery particles that swell
The changing volumes of the mingling streams,
The scenes reflected in their course but tell,
Such beauty would seem only true in dreams:
The graceful hills with various foliage clad,
The sunny meads with modest flowers besprent,
Gardens well trimmed with floral splendors glad,
Orchards, each branch with luscious burdens bent,
   And happy childhood dabbling in the tide,
   The wise and good that stroll along the side;

The dewy morns, when birds are blithely singing,
And many-tinted blossoms scent the breeze,
The buttercups from verdant meadows springing,
Mantles of tender foliage deck the trees;
Lilacs, in fragrance with the hawthorn vying,
Tulips their variegated splendors flaunt,
The modest mayflower 'neath the thicket lying,
Each floral sister in her favorite haunt,
  As genial spring, with love and beauty crowned,
  Diffuses life and growth on all around.

In my own youth how many a happy day
Seemed here all sunshine, all the rest forgot;
The garden ground with floral splendors gay,
Or lush with plum and peach and apricot;
The trellises with crowded clusters teem,
Edged round with box, the plots with berries spread;
Half hid by leaves the juicy seckels gleam,
And mellow apples fall, of gold and red, —
  In all that Eden, neither fruit nor flowers,
  If only ripe and asked for, but were ours:

Those pleasant rooms which on that garden look,
Wachuset in the west, that closed the scene,
The lawns and fields that sloped towards the brook,
The chestnut groves that flecked the meadow green,

The raft we slowly paddled round the pond,
Mysterious woods explored with timid tread,
Or traced the stream to the broad lake beyond,
In shady nook romantic legends read;
  When, wet and cold, we burrowed in the hay
  For eggs, beneath the rafters worked our way.

That spacious barn, — how well do I recall
Its empty mangers where whole herds might feed,
Unused, except one solitary stall
Where chewed the cud a cow of noble breed;
And, more remote, two steeds as raven black,
Indian and Prince, to many a memory dear;
As many more, which from the well-stored rack
Champed in companionship their well-earned cheer:
  The whole constructed round a cloistered square
  Which, swept and garnished, lay in silence
    there.

Within its mouldering walls a colt was foaled,
Whose sire at Ascot distanced all the field;
His graceful form, his temper kind and bold,
From eye to fetlock noblest blood revealed;
His frolic limbs, subdued as years rolled on,
Swift as the wind his early playmate bore;
They winged their way, the horse and rider one,

Along the Charles, whose streams, for miles a score,
  Nonantum's, Newton's paradise enclose,
  Which for their dwelling-place its patriarchs
    chose.

Lo, where beneath the breezes crisp the lake
Bearing a name remotest times well know,
Where all the birds the thirst of morning slake,
Its limpid depths with golden azure glow.
There float the lilies; near, the berries blush;
Perchance some maid unborn there con thy line,
From whose melodious flow rich fancies gush,
As these sweet waters from some source divine;
  Perchance thy poet form these shadows haunt,
  As thy inspired lays the world enchant.

As breaks the dawn, the silvery vapors float,
The rooster crows, the clucking hens draw near,
The Christmas gobbler clears his husky throat,
And echoes back the lusty chanticleer;
The lowing herds rush frantic from the barn,
The cow, impatient, bids the milkmaid haste,
The hungry spider spins his long-drawn yarn,
Unwary insects in his web enlaced;
  From every farm-house chimney curls the smoke,
  And savory rashers appetite provoke.

The ploughman chirrups as he drives his team,
His oxen gravely bending to their task,
Their fragrant breath reflects the bright'ning beam
In whose congenial warmth they fondly bask;
The harrow smooths the furrows, and the seed
He scatters broadcast, or in hill he drops,
And carefully eradicates each weed
May steal the richness from the looked-for crops;
  Then, all complete, regards with pride his field,
  And prays devoutly for a generous yield.

Who, at day-dawn, his native force renewed,
Dashes the dew-drops from the shrub and turf,
Ranges with quickened pulse the pathless wood,
Or breasts the breakers in the rolling surf;
Who rides, well-mounted, over hill and dale,
With rushing tramp speeds gayly o'er the beach,
On mountain-top hears, rising from the vale,
The village chimes and all their carols teach,
  But feels within his throbbing breast a sense
  Of something telling of omnipotence?

From out the parish church the pastor came,
A welcome guest, although his graces long;
He bore a name not quite unknown to fame,
Though given more to sermon than to song;

For sixty years he led his people up
Through tribulation to the skies above;
Orphans and widows shared his roof and cup, —
Their sole return, and all he wished, their love.
  If called eccentric, by the world decried,
  He was most free from selfishness and pride.

Too oft where wealth erects its castle wall
Towering in grandeur over all below,
When most elate it totters to its fall,
No vestige left, where once it stood, to show.
Upon yon hill, which overhangs the lake,
The lord of vast domains once reared his hold;
What fortune gives, some sad reverse may take;
There, now, the faith that John the Baptist told
  Is taught by shepherds like the honored seers,
  Who washed from ignorance its vice and tears.

Beyond, where woods and fields alternate spread,
Dwells Cincinnatus, who for freedom fought,
Brave men to victory had bravely led,
And many a laurel won that came unsought;
Now, in declining years, content to till
His fertile farms, extending far and wide;
All that love justice paying homage still
To one whom public clamor had belied, —

Clamor, that heeds not what it wounds or rends,
Rarely retracts, more rarely makes amends.

Trenton and Monmouth, Stony Point, to Wayne,
His youthful ardor, dauntless courage, test;
When public service needed him again,
He wisely ruled the regions farthest west;
Then came reproach, that heaviest cross to bear,
Perhaps less poignant when so undeserved, —
McLellan, Porter, Warren, forced to share,
The land ungrateful, which they nobly served;
    To all, at last, the vindication comes, —
    No better solace for their saddened homes.

Hull lived to see the friends that stood aloof
Come trooping back to grasp his genial hand,
To have him, best of all, beneath his roof
Who came, when both were young, from foreign
    land,
Left wife and child, and all that rank and wealth
Possessed to gratify the pride of life;
Prompted by noblest instincts, came by stealth
To aid in need, and share our doubtful strife, —
    Came now, our grateful nation's honored guest,
    To press once more each comrade to his
    breast.

The ways of God no human eyes discern, —
We must implore His care, and ask no more;
For conscience' sake the martyrs fearless burn,
From out their ashes to His presence soar;
What matters it that these frail forms of clay
May wince or groan with pain in every nerve;
That hearts may ache as too fond hopes betray?
Whate'er our lot, that lot we well deserve;
    Let us accept such cheer as Heaven ordains,
    For such brief period as of life remains.

The noble Bradstreet, who the farm possessed,
Entered with fearless step his prison cell;
When duty called him, craved nor peace nor rest,
Nor cared what doom his aged form befell.
He lived to see the tyrant take his place,
While he ruled wisely in that tyrant's stead;
Those that had wronged his country, in disgrace;
His country's love, to bless his dying bed, —
    What signified, when thus his course was run,
    Its many trials since its course begun?

The legend runs, that in his early youth
He bought the country round, for six poor kine,
Of saintly Mayhew, sent to teach the truth
To Vineyard Indians, moved by will divine.

It passed to Fuller, one remembered yet,
Who moulders not, his body self-embalmed;
Enduring as the fame of Margaret,
In battle dauntless, and whom shipwreck calmed.
　From this stanch stock Hull took his land and
　　bride,
　And now, near by, they slumber side by side.

CANTO VI.

THE FALLS OF THE CHARLES.

THE streams that drain this continent of ours,
 The overflow of our vast inland lakes,
In mighty cataracts their torrent pours;
Niagara the earth's foundations shakes;
Trenton's ribbed chambers with its amber flow,
And Minnehaha genius sanctifies;
Or Montmorenci, hoar with ice and snow,
Tulloola's thundering down 'neath southern skies,—
 Man dares not yet their majesty profane,
 Or desecrate God's altars for his gain.

Well might we wish like reverence would spare
Our waters, plunging headlong in their foam,
Or Edinburgh with us her Roslin share,
Her Arthur's Seat, for idle folk to roam.
But Nature 's for our sordid need defaced,
Our streams are valueless except for power;
Upon their brink some tasteless structure placed,
Whose lofty walls in ugly plainness tower

O'er meaner dwellings clustering beside, —
Eddies which fester in concealment glide.

Falls of the Charles, when Eliot first beheld,
How clothed with strength, how exquisite in
    grace!
Not one of all their boundless forests felled,
Save one lone wigwam, near no human trace;
The hurrying waters rushed, or plunged at will
In swirling eddies, and with cheery splash
The swollen currents all their channels fill,
Then down the ledge with force resistless crash;
    Flecked with their foam, as countless steeds in
        fight,
    They proudly swept, exultant in their might.

Thus through the tides of time its tireless way
It vigorously pursues in varying course;
The seasons change, primeval woods decay,
It presses on with unabated force;
At night about its bed the starry skies,
Save the lost Pleiad, roll in clustered throng;
The circling hills above the valley rise;
Steadfast, like them, the river hastes along
    Its several atoms to the boundless sea,
    Itself an emblem of eternity.

Winthrop, lest France should raid his infant home,
His trustiest scouts t' explore the country sends,
To build a stronghold should the Frenchmen come;
Three leagues above, where Charles with Mystic
    blends,
Where the bent river into bay expands,
Beat down by winter thaw and summer rains,
A battery the near approach commands, —
Trace of its ditch and rampart still remains;
    And where along the stream more safe retreat,
    Should Shawmut be assailed by hostile fleet?

Five generations earlier Columbus came,
Within the decade Cabot, Elyot, Thorne,
Explored the region round, gave it a name,
Which from that time it ever since has borne.
Cartier, Champlain, and pilots of the best,
Studied out the bays and inlets along shore;
Traded with savages for furs and fish,
Passed up the rivers both with sail and oar,
    Though not too certain where their sandfall lay,
    Or Norumbega stretched its devious way.

Enough to know, from various traces still
Of ponds dammed up, embankments overgrown,
The white man wandered over vale and hill,

Left many a mark for us a marvel still;
From what they left in print or manuscript,
Conviction clear they hither came to dwell,
Measuring their courses as the magnet dipt,
Until, it may be, some mischance befell;
    Experts assert they surely found such site
    At Weston, where Stony Brook and Charles
      unite.

Yet civilization since has changes wrought, —
The river dammed, the saw-mill's hungry maw
Devoured the wood the patient oxen brought,
Where grimy foundries shaped the ductile ore;
And now a vast infinitude of wheels
Attire the naked, and the hungry feed;
And all that man has done, or thought, or feels,
His wits discovered, or his fancies breed,
    Is scattered broadcast, on the leaves impressed
    Of Newton's pulpy fabric, deemed the best.

Midst the dark shadows of an ancient forge,
All the more picturesque, — no rules control, —
Below the bridge the waters gain a gorge,
Between whose cliffs precipitous they roll;
With bushes draped, the vale in breadth expands,
Its bed descends till partly lost to sight;

Midst tangled growth the lofty hemlock stands,
The rapid slopes the snow-wreath flecks with white;
　The woods and rocks, the grand and lovely blend,
　The widespread streams beyond new beauty lend.

From all these tasks, less limpid than before,
The river, shrunk through flumes and sluices, glides
Over the dam; its yeasty flood no more
Falls toppling.　Part in rocky caverns hides
Beneath the conduit which the Sudbury brings;
The rest fills full the span where echo dwells,
Mocking the voice that cheers, or shouts, or sings;
The arch with Indian war-whoops rings, or yells,
　To fade away in moan, or sob, or sigh,
　As their heroic shades flit sadly by.

Within that bright expanse, in calm repose,
The Charles recruits its vigor for its work;
Its shore around, the clustered homes enclose,
The shameless inns where lazy loiterers lurk,
The church where Baurie taught his loving flock,
Smithies that tire the wain or fashion shoes,
The country store, with multifarious stock,
Distributes letters and retails the news,
　Where eager gossips come for chat or mirth,
　And mutual liking ripens into birth.

Brooks that amidst the lofty mountains nursed,
Fed on the avalanche, in volume grow;
Broad, swift, and deep, their icy fetters burst
To hurl destruction upon all below;
The peaceful Charles, with no such mischief fraught,
The ponds that feed it regulate its flow,
Neither by flood nor drought such havoc wrought,
For those in peril, times and seasons know;
  Set ope the gates, when dangerous its course,
  That on the widespread meadows spends its force.

Thrice blessed the town grouped round some
      pent-up stream,
With force to help in all its various tasks,
Where day and night the cheerful lustres beam,
And labor gains the bread it daily asks;
If, like kind Providence, it sometimes frown
Should drought diminish, or advancing spring
Midst all the showers and freshets raging down,
Against the dam their ponderous fury fling,
  Science and care keep guard to thwart the foe,
  Struggling in vain to work to overthrow.

Nor men nor river can be always gay;
Its pent-up waters, rushing down the flume,
Doffed gala garb; the maids, in plain array,

Keep to their task the spindle and the loom,
To bless the world with cleanliness and health;
For these old mills stood foremost in the van
When public spirit ventured all its wealth
To set us free from that leviathan,
    Who, like old Saturn that devoured his sons,
    Would clothe the subject nations with her guns.

We had been kindred near a thousand years,
Her strifes and struggles had been ours to share;
But love grows cold when power domineers,
And scorn and wrong not hers or ours to bear.
From 'neath our flag her cruisers wrenched the
       crew,
Our ships, unmanned, condemned to hopeless
       wreck;
We were no cowards, and the sword we drew,
And fought our quarrel on her bloody deck,
    Till her proud arms, victorious no more,
    Discomfited, from off our shores withdraw.

We could not trust her, with her greed and pride,
Nor brook dependence on her craft or skill;
Peace has its triumphs, and upon the Clyde,
As round the world, the clash of arms grew still;
With mutual pledge, two generous men resolved

Their native land from foreign yoke to free,
And as in tribulation years revolved,
One lived, at least, that pledge made good to see ;
  And these old mills their wisdom earliest planned,
  Still by the Charles, to speak their praises,
    stand.

Yet if from greed, thus pitiless, we wrest
The right our garments for ourselves to weave,
We still can mourn for fellow-men distressed,
Who, their vocation gone, must sorely grieve
That what we gain, their breadless children doom
To exile from the home they prize so dear,
Compels their race to an untimely tomb,
For the survivors left a future drear :
  · Such over Switzerland the cloud that lowers,
  Since Waltham watches measure all the hours.

The rush of waters from the falls above,
Impeded in their course by rocks below,
Expand their fretted force in many a cove,
Then, gathering in their might, resistless flow
In chasing torrents down the steep incline,
Leaping the rocky ledge with deaf'ning roar,
Nor miss the portion which, on quest benign,
With gentler motion glides along the shore

To turn the wheels our earliest fabrics wove,
Or work some saw-mill in a neighb'ring grove.

From poet's lake, fair Rosemary in aid,
Their mingled waters thence with quick'ning sweep
Within two leagues, in rapid or cascade,
Dash down two hundred feet, and in one leap
Twenty at least, to furnish useful power,
For many a happy home creating wealth,
Imparting moisture to the tree and flower,
To thirsty cities bringing joy and health;
    By villas, groves, and garden grounds they glide,
    Nor pause for rest till they reach Riverside.

CANTO VII.

WHERE once the dusky brave his bark canoe
　　Let float in stillness lest it fright the deer,
With aim unerring prowling panthers slew,
Or from his ambush marked his foe draw near,
In proud array the homes of affluence,
Complete in all that wealth and art combine
To gratify the taste or please the sense,
Each from the rest concealed, the river line;
　With vistas through the branches to the stream
　Whose rippling wavelets in the noonday gleam.

When the full moon is up, the summer eve,
Each ripple on the surface fret with gold,
The boughs that fringe the shores their shadows
　　　weave,
And spectral forms their fleecy vestures fold;
Still, save the wash that lulls the unconscious ear,
Some baying dog, or chance some curfew bell,

Wakes whispered echoes from the hillsides near,
Whose quiet hush soothes back the broken spell,
  The earth around in vestal beauty lies,
  And angel wings fan fresh this paradise.

No eye can see, and sure no tongue would tell
The happy hours that men and maids have known;
In strolls along the banks or neighboring dell,
Or floating on the stream, the hours have flown;
The jocund voice of childhood at its sport,
Friendship, than which no greater boon can bless,
The fancies fond from airy nothings wrought,
That sense of life, itself a happiness, —
  Where'er we roam, such memories attend,
  And dull realities their glamour lend.

Upon the cliffs whose rapid slope declines
In curve and terrace to the marge below,
A lady bright, who taste with sense combines,
And gift to teach all that is good to know,
Has perched her nest for callow maids to learn
Whatever can adorn or elevate,
Kind friends endear, or just approval earn,
And be contented though unfortunate;
  With skill like hers to form the heart and mind,
  Far less the chance that Fortune prove unkind.

Within the nook below, ensconced from view,
Where placid waters brim the grassy mead,
These opening buds their various ends pursue, —
Sing with the birds, alternate verses read;
Should warmth persuade, their sheltered bath is
      near,
For many a life prolonged for those that swim;
They ply the rod or oar, adroitly steer
Their shapely skiffs, and then with agile limb,
  As lengthening shadows falling dew-drops warn,
  Climb up the cliff for tennis on the lawn.

In feudal days man's lawless violence
Drove to the cloister all that were not strong;
The Church, forgiving much to penitence,
Chose the most precious from the spoils of wrong;
Where best the soil and scene, the convent bell
Measured in music all the peaceful hours,
The lovely mynchens learned their beads to tell,
With many a secret from the birds and flowers;
  And when their beauty ruled in camp and court,
  The world improved from what the convent
    taught.

To play the harp, list to the troubadour,
Embroider tapestry for bower and hall,

To ride to hounds, or guide the falcon's soar,
Beguiled the maid no vanities enthrall;
But now, to know all science, speak each tongue,
All faiths, philosophies, to comprehend,
To sing the airs the latest Diva sung, —
These, and much else, in modern culture blend;
    And sure, no fitter spot, no safer guides,
      Than Wellesley's, or Lassell's, or Riverside's.

Each brook and brake, each rock and floweret wild,
The budding mind some precious wisdom teach;
A taste for Nature planted in the child
Grows with its growth, and joys beyond the reach
Of adverse fortune yields from youth to age;
It lends to character another charm,
New warmth and life to the historic page,
Disarms romance of all its power to harm;
    And, as we learn the universal plan,
      The simpler seems God's providence to man.

Not always undisturbed, the sons of toil
Dapple the river's breadth with frequent oar,
And swarms of sail-boats up its current coil,
Wooing the adverse breeze from shore to shore;
And steamers, gay with pennon and with song,
Pour forth sweet melodies from happy throats,

And as the motley concourse speeds along,
Chorus or hymn upon the moonlight floats;
   And flute and clarinet some tender strain
   Breathe softly forth, — then all is mute again.

Or when, upon our country's natal day
The wheels stand still, the idle river free
Rolls on unchecked, as rollic boys at play,
And all alike delight in liberty;
Some gaze from Prospect o'er the views superb,
The elders solemn services enjoy,
While youth, whose soul no carking cares disturb,
Upon the stream they love the fish decoy;
   Or, in the shady woods that line the bank,
   Make merry in the dance or frolic prank.

Upon a point which juts into the broad,
Where the Charles, bending, forms a spacious cove,
Mid stately drives and widely spreading sward,
With groves and clumps that interarch above,
A noble mansion stands, of faultless form
And exquisite proportions, white as snow;
Yet more substantial to resist the storm,
Its walls of stone in gorgeous sunset glow;
   Sumptuous within, sure nowhere to be found
   A lovelier Eden than the scene around.

The crystal panes that span the windows wide
Command for miles the river and its shore;
From its own boat-house yacht and steamer glide,
And vigorous muscles ply the rival oar;
When frosty days the neighb'ring youth entice,
What rosy throngs skate rushingly along!
As night grows cold, how booms the stiff'ning ice,
What shouts of laughter and what floods of song!
   And jingling bells, perchance, as well-filled
     sleighs
   Speed swiftly by upon the snow-clad ways!

Or when fast-falling flakes obscure the sky,
And trees and shrubs to sheeted spectres change,
The eddying flurries pile the drifts on high,
And wrap the earth in silence weird and strange;
Should thaw and frost o'er all their magic throw,
And morning sunshine flood the vale with light,
Its beams resplendent from the crusted snow,
Each branch and twig ablaze with crystals bright,
   No Eblis hall from Orient's fabled tale
   Excels in dazzling beauty hill and dale.

Behold from Prospect's brow the sunbeams play
On stream and forest, spread in beauty round,
On lofty peaks full thirty leagues away

Gleaming like gems upon the horizon's bound;
Or where, less far, Monadnock proudly soars,
And nearer yet, Wachusett, girt with lakes;
While close at hand the noontide splendor pours
A purple sheen that Massasoit takes
  And shares with Bellevue, Corey, and Wauban,
  With Newton's seven hills, and Natick's Mount
    Pegan.

Or from Mount Feake observe the clustered throng,
Cities and towns a-swarm with happy souls,
Sails from whose looms waft the big ships along
Through gates of Charles, where boundless ocean
    rolls;
There grinds the lens that guides the skipper's sight,
Others that shield the beacons down the shore,
The helmsman's compass, binnacle with light,
Or help astronomers the skies explore;
  No distant orb, space tenantless or dark,
  Unknown to science, through these disks of Clark.

The useful arts, that all the thoughts employ,
Lend wings to life with every duty done,
Toil and repose no anxious cares annoy,
A calm content that mourns no day has gone;
The sober sense, by honest labor earned,
That we have bravely played our part below,

From every trouble all its wisdom learned,
And paid to God and man each debt we owe;
  With gratitude for all our blessings here,
  Without regret when death's dark shadows near.

Such the reward when, true to Nature's laws,
Our several tasks performed with pious trust,
Without ambition for the world's applause,
Our words and deeds all generous and just;
What though our lot be humble, — simplest toil,
Where lofty motive prompts, is sanctified;
No menial labors can the soul assoil
That food or raiment for our homes provide;
  We live, we learn, we love, we plant and reap,
  Then with our fathers in the churchyard sleep.

These the blest homes which every virtue grace,
Such the enchantments meet the daily view,
Each season brings its pleasures in their place,
And all their cherished memories renew;
Along the margin, in sequestered spots,
Moulder the ashes of the loved and lost,
Where modest daisies and forget-me-nots
Return each spring and in the zephyrs tossed
  Beside the grave, to those that loved and live,
  Of life beyond their soothing presage give.

All honor to the man of noble soul
Endowed by Providence with will and wealth
To take like care of all in his control,
Will best promote their comfort and their health;
Nor only this, — but generously provides
All such conditions as their lives can bless,
Such harmless recreations, and besides
Such sweet affections as his own possess,
   With tastes and culture, and that moral sense
   That lends its highest worth to competence.

This the intent, and such the practice too
Adopted when these Waltham works were reared;
If not in all, the good example grew,
Nor has as yet its influence disappeared;
Its people temperate, pure, intelligent,
Noted for thrift, obedient to the law,
With what vouchsafed their grateful hearts content,
Nor wasting what they have by lust for more;
   And such must be the general happiness,
   Should all but practise what they now profess.

What life so sad as that of idleness?
Not all the luxuries that gold can buy,
No pride of health, or strength, or comeliness,
Or art, or Nature's charms, can satisfy,

Unless ambition, appetite, and greed
Stir mind and nerve to vig'rous exercise,
One task accomplished to another lead,
And each in turn attain its wished-for prize;
  Unless each day in due proportion given
  To work and well-earned rest, — to earth and
    heaven.

Go ask the school-boy, who amidst his tasks
Yearned for vacation that he might be free,
When now in pampered ease at last he basks,
And seeks delight in dull satiety,
If half as happy his long holiday
As when his lessons occupied his thought,
And fixed attention whirled the hours away,
Till all made clear the problem that he wrought;
  How gladly now would he those tasks resume, —
  That busy round that spares no time for gloom!

Or hear the rich man's son, whose ample store
Closes for him the avenues of trade,
The healing art, the pulpit, and the law,
Or work as useful, if of lowlier grade;
When all explored the earth's remotest nooks,
Traversed the paths each traveller pursues,
Sated with pictures, wearied with his books,

And half their joys his social pleasures lose,
  With downcast look the saddening truth confess
  How worthless gold to purchase happiness.

No need to test, to learn no life of ease,
Of mere amusement, can the spirit sate;
What man calls pleasure soonest fails to please,
Intensest joys are speediest to grate;
Yet toil continual, no repose, relief,
Thwarts quite as much intent of Providence,
That mingles in each life both joy and grief, —
The pleased content, and then the aching sense;
  Gives work and rest, depression and delight,
  The hope, the fear, — the day, and then the night.

The church, the school, the court-room and parade,
The choral class with simple psalm and song,
To frame one's house, which neighbors troop to aid,
And social huskings that all ages throng;
The bee that hives the honey, clothes the poor,
The sugar-camps whose fragrant caldrons steam,
The rustic reel, which shakes the cottage floor,
Saw-mill and cider-press and troutful stream, —
  These simple pleasures, mingling work and play,
  Drive off dull care and wing the hours away.

HOMES OF WEALTH.

NOT far below, a broad domain enchants,
　　The fleecy clouds the lawn with shadows fleck,
The sturdy oak that age primeval vaunts,
And graceful elms the dimpled surface deck;
Vistas of sunny glades in distance lost
Mid foliage dense, or rising knoll, reveal
Some startled deer that nimbly flit across
Till checked by tether that the leaves conceal;
　　Or else some shady seat in rustic bower,
　　For social converse or an idle hour.

Not without record here the Garfields grew,
Here felled the forest, tilled the fertile soil;
Their busy feet brushed off the morning dew,
And golden plenty blessed their rudest toil;
When the third patriarch, full of honors, dead,
His numerous scions sold their home away,
Sought for new pastures by Otsego's head,
Where they successive generations stay;

Where lived and loved the parents of a son
Whose life and death the world-wide plaudits won.

For services in Senate and on field,
With one acclaim we chose him for our chief;
Too resolute one jot to favor yield,
An angered madman plunged the land in grief;
All Christendom, not our land alone,
Beside his pillow watched with hopes and fears;
The world, responsive to his dying moan,
In that great sorrow all dissolved in tears,
    They mourned the man who was thus truly great,
    The nation's loss, not for his pride of state.

Amidst these grounds a stately mansion stands,
With many precious memories that cling;
Its earliest lord, when sent to foreign lands
On public service to his whilom king,
Received the tidings that his ancient home
Had fallen victim to consuming flames;
And on its site his speedy orders come
For this, resembling one upon the Thames;
    In elegance and comfort not surpassed,
    Its solid walls for centuries to last.

Its marble hall, about whose ample board
Near forty kinsfolk sat in fellowship;

Its oval presence-room, as high and broad,
Where old and young in country dances trip;
Parlors that taste and cosiness combined;
Billiards for healthy exercise in rain;
That library, with precious volumes lined,
The wise most covet, or great wealth obtain;
　　Such for long years the hospitable home
　　Of friends and kindred who were pleased to come.

Around the borders of this fair domain,
Within encircling woods, the long-drawn aisle,
When summer noonday scorches all the plain,
With shaded strolls the sleepy hours beguile;
Kennel and stall hold many a loving friend;
The dairy trim with cooling freshness dight;
And mingled fragrance pinks and roses lend
To lade the zephyr or the bees delight;
　　And warblers carol, and the raven rook
　　Caws from the shelter of his leafy nook.

And certainly no better monument,
More durable, or useful to their kind,
Than such abode with its environment, —
If their desire to be borne in mind.
But Gore, the statesman and the much-beloved,
In troubled times our State's chief magistrate,

Gave Harvard College, which he fondly loved,
A liberal portion of his large estate:
   This built the noble hall that bears his name,
   And holds its library well known to fame.

'T is sad to think, as generations pass,
How frail the tenure that they have of earth,
That those who most their fellow-men surpass
In noble traits, in character or worth,
When at their best fade from the world away,
Leaving rich memories for the few to mourn;
Or — cheering hope — death harbingers a day
Of which existence here is but the dawn;
   How brief the years that carried to the skies
   Six souls who dearly loved this paradise!

Who does not long at times the crowd to shun,
To rest from pleasure as one rests from care,
Feel painful sense of duties left undone,
Yearn with their fellow-men their tasks to share?
To soul devout, when some affliction wrings
The heart with anguish and the skies grow drear,
From out their clouds some angel whisper brings
The surest solace, others' woe to cheer.
   Greene left his home, the priestly garb put on,
   And found his peace by Christian service won.

Life for the happiest is not alway joy,
The brightest sky the darkest clouds obscure,
And Nature's laws both sun and shower employ,
The stormiest winds the sturdiest growth insure;
If pain and sorrow make us more like Him
Who died on earth that we may live in heaven,
What though our eyes with tears at times grow dim,
Or we on wintry seas are tempest-driven,
 If with firm faith, whatever ill betide,
 His helping spirit hover at our side?

On few bestowed by loving Providence
In larger measure all this world makes bright, —
Warm heart, high principle, and keenest sense
Of what is loveliest or what is right;
Congenial sympathies brought hosts of friends,
Affection fond those nearest more endeared,
With all that culture, taste, or wisdom lends
To form a character that all revered.
 Greene in this home for many summers dwelt,
 Both loved and lost, — both joy and sorrow felt.

Not yet forgot that night of mantling snow,
Bright in the moonbeams glimmering far and wide;
In the huge sleigh the ruddy faces glow
Of lads and maidens seated side by side,

When rippling converse loving souls attune
To the romantic beauty of the night,
Till merrier glees and rushing steeds too soon
Bring to the festal hall of warmth and light;
    There at its heaped-up board of fruit and flowers
    We laughed away the gay and happy hours.

Nor yet that monthly club, when comrades dear
We gathered at the banquet, and each kind
Of pear or apple crowned the ample cheer
From his own trees; famed wines the buffet lined;
Where Warren, Hooper, merry doctors sat,
Motley and Sargent, famous with the pen,
Bryant and Dwight, with ever lively chat,
And courteous Dutton, prince of gentlemen;
    And Sullivan, with fun in endless store,
    Like Yorick, kept the table in a roar.

Nor yet those summer days when balmy breeze,
That Flora loads with fragrance and delight,
Ripples the clover, rustles in the trees,
As the still gloaming settles into night.
Surely none kinder than that gracious dame,
No host more courteous than her genial son,
Her life the brighter for the world-wide fame
Her father's genius and her brother's won;

And manly bishop, both with whip and crook,
Repeated noblest verse from poet's book.

Across the Charles, Greene found a loving flock;
He built their church and gave his life to them,
The best of comfort from the Living Rock,
For earthly cross a heavenly diadem.
When his own health no longer left him strength
For parish charge, and others took his place,
He still his Master served; and when at length
In humble trust he closed his earthly race,
   Sure none can doubt, with faith that God is love,
   His name inscribed in the great book above.

With equal scales the honored Themis came,
And none than he more conversant with law;
From care and thought to rose and lilac came,
Athirst for Nature from his fast before;
His blood, commingled with our poet's bays,
Transmits his ermine to another Holmes,
Skilled as his grandsire in the darkling ways,
The lurid wisdom of black-letter tomes.
   The muse that Murray, Story loved, forsook,
   Illumines Saunders, Littleton, and Coke.

In our well-tempered clime, that lies midway
From pole to tropic, half our forests drop

Their annual leaves in beautiful decay;
The lofty pines upon the mountain-top,
Lest winter's winds should chill, their garb retain;
When axe or fire sweep either from the ground,
The mould can but its opposite sustain:
And thus through ages the alternate round,
From sire to son the electric fire descends,
And now a poet, now a jurist lends.

Who that recalls the frank and dauntless mien
Of that bold civic chief who, self-possessed,
Averted perils which then still unseen,
Our civil war a nation's blood repressed, —
That calm good sense and courteous dignity,
Wise plans that still promote the public good,
But ready tribute pay to memories
Which richly merit all our gratitude;
His duty done, his useful work complete,
He found repose, well-earned, in this retreat.

Near, his paternal home, where taste and means
To make this pleasant world more pleasant yet
Transform to garden ground the rustic scenes,
Where snare for beaver once the huntsman set,
Where every stranger deemed of all the guest
Its various charms, of country round the pride,

6

The open gates their welcome warm expressed,
To none that could appreciate denied;
    Its kine, upon luxuriant pastures fed,
    Sent health and life to many a sick man's bed.

Now other generations bear the name
From such a sire and grandsire well derived.
One, when our streams and lakes had lost their fame
Of fish, once plentiful, but few survived,
By weirs and spawn, bass, salmon, shad, restored,
To feed the hungry, make the angler glad;
And with such service Charles may well record
Sargent's, who, mourning for the woods that clad
    This spacious land the centuries ago,
    Has bid its forests still again to grow.

Life runs apace.   No effort of our own
Can stay its progress, or give back the past;
Fond memory recalls its moments flown,
Its steps in clay, hardened to rock at last;
This lovely river, down whose course we float,
Takes its last plunge, then mingles with the tide;
Yet from its portals to its source remote
It alters not; through time its waters glide.
    Though man be mortal, still the race lives on;
    The soul survives though all of earth be gone.

CANTO IX.

NONANTUM from her hills across the stream,
    The region from its waters took its name, —
The happy scene of many a youthful dream,
And many there such memories can claim.
A statelier mansion occupies the site
Where one by all beloved, and near of kin,
By cordial welcome shed around the light
Of his own beaming soul on all within;
    Upon his spacious grounds, screened by the wood,
    A home in summer for his kinsfolk stood.

Belmont, in all its pristine beauty still,
If grander now, it was as charming then;
The same bright sunbeams all its chambers fill,
Its lawns and woods not lovelier than when
We freely roamed within its garden gate,
Where grapes and nect'rines ripened on the wall,
Beneath the oak and elm in joyance sat,
And shadows marked from quivering foliage fall;

Or on that matchless scene of beauty fed,
Which, miles around, in summer glamour spread.

It well deserved the name that Portia bore,
Which now attaches to the country round;
And others famed for beauty, by the score,
Blend all their charms in one vast pleasure-ground.
The road beyond, he of the silver lip
There grew to semblance of his rose and oak,
Nor bee nor bird could sweeter honey sip
Than melted into music when he spoke.
    The roses still their fragrant odors shed;
    That voice is hushed which once the Senate led.

Near by the margin of a crystal lake
Whose limpid waters quench the scholar's thirst;
Its nooks and coves all forms of beauty take,
Upon the eye with fresh enchantment burst.
Once through the genial season long drawn out
Here strolled, in pleased delight, three honored men,
Whose taste and means embellished all about,
With slopes of sunshine and sequestered glen;
    Yet, not content with scenes like these enjoyed,
    Their wealth for others generously employed.

Thus the proud race we claim to be our own
Live out their span, then moulder 'neath the sod;

Their souls still sentient pass to realms unknown,
With steadfast trust in their creating God;
Their life, transmitted, animates fresh forms,
Who in their turn spring up, mature, decay,
Enjoy life's blessings, strengthen with its storms,
Then in its sepulchres return to clay.
    The generations pass, the race still lives,
    Content to take what He in wisdom gives.

So flows the river down the sands of time;
The breeze restores the moisture to the hills,
The fleecy burdens up the valleys climb,
Then gayly ripple down their crystal rills;
Fill full the stream which rushes to the sea,
Buffet its currents, mingle with its brine,
Shrink, timid, back from its immensity,
Till, downward swept where no more shores confine,
    They feel in glad amaze their boundless form,
    Play with its monsters, battle with its storm.

The dead rest 'neath the sod, the dew-drops in the
      deep;
Before us sweeps the river, freshened by the tide
Daily its briny currents flood, then downward
      creep
As we upon its waves in contemplation glide;

Wide its humid marshes, swift flows its swollen
    stream,
The forest hoar primeval spreads its gnarlèd boughs,
While amidst their foliage homes of affluence
    gleam,
The dainty flocks are nibbling and herds of cattle
    browse;
    What tales these homes might tell of honored
      lives well spent,
    Of mingled joy and sorrow alike in kindness sent!

On the right bank, towards the sunny south,
What once was country, now but suburb drear,
Where hill and dale teemed with luxuriant growth,
The noisy workshops sooty chimneys rear.
One glory left; long famous for the speed
Elastic turf or smoothest road incite,
The honors won by many a well-known steed
All that love horses give supreme delight;
    Their glistening eyes, their vigorous pulses beat
    With quickened glow at each contested heat.

Who the midwinter, as the sun goes down,
And all the skies are flushed with iris hues,
With all the Jehus' roadsters of renown,
Hies eager on ahead of him pursues,

Strives hard to gain on him that flies before,
While sleighs and double sleighs of gold and green,
And sleigh-bells ring, and lusty voices roar,
Will soon forget that animated scene,
 As all that rapid throng one torrent flowed
 Hilarious along the Brighton road?

Here Faneuil, Parsons, made their summer home
When heated city drove them to the field;
Now their old mansions tempt no more to roam,
Their lawns and gardens to improvement yield;
Woods made for them a wilderness of shade,
The long-drawn aisles and terraces of pride,
Their beauty gone, are avenues of trade,
Of tasteless dwellings crowded side by side;
 The sylvan paths, where gentle neighbors meet,
 Dusty beneath the tramp of busy feet.

Much we may mourn the ravage in its path,
The desolation of utility;
Indignant Nature veils her face in wrath,
For aught unseemly has no eyes to see;
Still, yonder rail that spans the continent
Permits a thousand live where one before;
What though the plains be scarred, the forest rent,
If man be multiplied still more and more, —

If fifty millions may in comfort dwell,
Our gloated pride among the nations swell?

Many still living were to manhood grown
When this great marvel did not yet exist,
Its wondrous possibilities unknown,
Blessings no human presage yet had missed.
Now Vulcan weaves such network round the world
In jealous rage he forged for Beauty's queen,
Forgets not why his cruel mother hurled
From heaven to hell through all the span between;
    Revenge is sweet, and now his turn to mar
    The realms of beauty with unsightly scar.

So here along the bank, as slopes the cliff,
Longwood for miles stretched in majestic grace,
Its various growths beheld from knoll or cliff
Lends a most stately presence to the place.
Above the girding woods, with forest crowned,
Soars in its grand proportions Corey's hill;
In all these solitudes of shade but found
One mouldering farm-house that was dwelt in still.
    Perhaps the same, among the centuries flown,
    In the warm season Sewall made his own.

His faithful gardens still their place retain,
Pear-trees descended from his veteran stock;

His vigorous oaks o'erspread the dimpled plain,
From out the turf protrudes the stubborn rock.
Here, on the morn that ushered in the fight
On Bunker Hill shook off our foreign yoke,
Warren, who that day perished for the right,
Rested his steed while his last fast he broke;
    Prescott's own post, which led that band of braves
    So soon to slumber in their honored graves.

Here affluence, prompted by no sordid aim,
Fills up the marsh, the ragged pasture clears,
Merits the praise it will not stoop to claim,
So richly won by Lawrence and by Sears, —
One motive, doubtless, to enlarge their wealth.
Their cheerful dwellings other men enjoy,
Hundreds live blessed with elegance and health,
Their scantier means in other ways employ, —
    Securing comfort for the child and wife,
    Plenty and peace beyond the strifes of life.

Few selfish fences bar the wish to range,
All freely ramble through the field and wood;
The dogs may bark if aught uncouth or strange
Upon this peaceful paradise intrude;
The spacious lawns in turfy verdure spread,
Rare flowers and shrubs its gay parterre adorn,

Blossoms and buds their spicy odors shed;
And as the springtide ushers in the morn
    Of a new growth, trees don their proud parade
    To cool the summer heats with grateful shade.

Surely no spot along the river's bank
Can boast, for souls refined, a home more blessed;
Even Muddy River's waters grow less rank,
Quickened their course, by wooded cliffs com-
        pressed;
Up its long vale a pleasure park will soon
Attract who love the grace to Nature given,
By taste prepared for all the precious boon
Of rural beauty canopied by heaven, —
    Of boundless woods, of dingle, ledge, and lake,
    That all the weary-laden may partake.

Not in our day, perhaps, the whole complete:
Cycles of time the works of man perfect;
Not ours, but time's, who speeds with rapid
        feet
To curve the slopes, the graceless line correct,
To grow the trees, and mat their foliage dense,
Embalmed by beauty ever to delight;
Nor time's work only, but Omnipotence,
That shapes, creates, to gratify our sight;

From homes above we too may witness be
Of all made perfect living men may see.

Who, musing, strolls along the river side,
This wealth of woodland pauses to survey,
Across the Charles, there flowing deep and wide,
The morning beams on tower and steeple play,
And all that stately growth in radiance steep
Down to the brink in matted masses crowds,
All still, save where the filmy shadows creep,
Dropped idly down from out the passing clouds,—
   Can gaze unmoved, or turn away his eyes
   Riveted upon the spot in pleased surprise?

Above the tree-tops soaring to the sky
Tower and spire reared reverently to God,
Beneath their sacred walls the ashes lie
Of many a noble breast, beneath the sod.
Two loving brothers, children of a saint,
Their spotless lives the Sermons on the Mount;
In deeds of charity nor fail nor faint,
Both sire and sons recording angels count
   In their own books of souls by love redeemed,
   Whose fellow-mortals, all who knew, esteemed.

And who can doubt the purposes of God
Exemplified in saintly souls like theirs?

Their much-loved forms may crumble 'neath the
    sod,
More fitting homes He up above prepares;
Prophets and miracles and sacred creeds
Guided their footsteps, in His image formed;
Pure in their hearts and generous in their deeds,
Their kindly natures by His spirit warmed.
  New generations, by His mercy blest,
  Will find beside His throne their heavenly rest.

The dewy gossamer on the morning turf
Melts in the fountain, brimmeth in the sea,
Restless and fretful in the storm-tost surf,
Ever the same throughout eternity.
Vapor or avalanche or rock-ribbed ice,
It weaves the garment or propels the ship;
If seeming valueless beyond all price
To soothe the anguish or to cool the lip,
  Guided by science, crushes adamant,
  Or, pent in coils, its vigorous pulses pant.

Genius, inventive, ponders out the laws,
Its secret treasuries develop force,
Its thoughtful meditations know no pause
Till put to use each limitless resource.
Its essence tells how tough and strong the bar,

In every engine every prop makes safe,
Puts at his ease the traveller in his car,
Adjusts each bearing that no friction chafe ;
   In noiseless beauty with amazement sees
   Weighed in its ponderous scales all energies.

CANTO X.

CAMBRIDGE.

TRADITION tells too of that other shore,
    In earlier times a wilderness of shade,
With verdant meadows spreading out before,
Below the level of the forest grades.
Here Dudley came, his spacious mansion reared
(Too grand, as Winthrop thought, for simple saints),
And many more, who soon the forest cleared,
Whom no such taste for worldly splendor taints;
    They felled the trees to build a palisade
    To guard the settlement from Indian raid.

That settlement composed of scattered farms,
Part of that Newtown twenty miles around,
Embraced, by tortuous Charles, within its arms
An ample space of far more fertile ground;
Here the wise fathers of the infant State
Planted their college, Harvard helped endow, —
Another Cambridge vying with its mate
In purpose then, in wealth and influence now;

Its crystal founts with wisdom, science flow,
To what effect our simple annals show.

While the colonial charter freedom sheds,
Charon alone gives access to this shrine;
When kings that sacred charter tore to shreds,
Phipps, who plucked fortune from beneath the
      brine,
And ruled these royal realms and Acadie,
Built the old bridge towards the college gate;
When one more century made us truly free,
The earliest governor of the new-born State
    In lordly pageant opened up the way
    All have since passed, on Harvard's gala day.

When our great-grandsires homage paid the Crown,
Above the bridge, along the western bank,
Dwelt a long line of magnates of renown,
In wealth and culture with the proudest rank;
Lechmeres and Vassals, Leonards, Olivers,
Who passed their days in luxury and ease,
Indifferent to the generous ardor stirs
The sons of freedom, whom their ways displease;
    The sable clouds big with the coming storm
    Why should they care? Their nests are snug
      and warm.

Below the college bridge as many more, —
Inman and Phipps and Apthorp and the rest,
Whose kindly souls and ever open door
Feasted their neighbors, succored the distrest.
The tempest burst, and loyal to their king
They steadfast stood, and met the exile's fate;
Their large domains but little comfort bring,
Sequestered or confiscate to the State;
   Their spacious mansions still the river line,
   Once rich in books, in plate, and luscious wine.

In regal days the heirs of opulence
Contented grouped about these college grounds,
Their graceful hospitality dispense,
Enhance the natural beauty that surrounds.
The same attraction when for freedom's sake,
No longer shackled, they their rulers chose;
Congenial tastes these homes deserted take,
And fond of learning find the like repose;
   These ancient mansions still their grace retain,
   Though names familiar once, now sought in vain.

Some were more prudent, sheltered from the gale
By loving friends, who saved them from the laws:
Brattle and Foster reefed the imperilled sail,
The country free, their large estates restores;

Some wise to see the spirit that prevailed
Must end in independence just and true,
With welcome mind each rebel victory hailed,
With each success their hopes of victory grew,
    Till, after years of tribulation dire,
    They lived to see all kingly rule expire.

Dana, among the first the hazard cast,
All through the war no change of purpose knew;
An honored judge, a statesman unsurpassed,
In useful service rivalled but by few.
Langdon, the president of the college, grave,
Stood at his post and fearless braved the storm,
Prayed with the men who gave their lives to save
Their menaced country from the hungry swarm
    Of British myrmidons, ordered to destroy
    Their heritage they knew not to enjoy.

Meanwhile our capital beleaguered lay;
Its garrison a mercenary horde,
All summer long their angry cannon play
Upon the rebels, who with one accord
Their homes and families left in holy trust,
Gathered around the town, their vigil kept
Lest well-armed foes should, like some sudden gust,
Assail them at advantage while they slept;

7

With less to fear, for Washington too wise
To expose his army to the least surprise.

His home still stands, the tasteful Vassal built,
Whose slave was idly swinging on the gate,
When, his sword sheathed, the General dropped
    the hilt,
Dismounted from his steed, and forced to wait
While the dark henchman urged to be employed,
And now a freedman bargained for his wage.

   .   .   .   .

Beneath its roof one day in counsel met
Ward, Lee, and Putnam, Thomas Knox and Gates,
Greene, Sullivan, Spenser, in due order set, —
In dire dismay, as commissary states
His make-believe of barrels filled with sand,
While all the powder he could rake and scrape
But forty charges for lines thinly manned,
From Mystic waters round to Squantum Cape:
    A solemn silence, seemed an age's length,
    Revealed our weakness and our foemen's strength.

Concealment pledged, and sages called in aid
From General Court at Watertown near by,
Swift couriers sent, whose course was never stayed

Till bold Revere from Congress brought supply;
Another day the General reached his door
To find the aged Putnam on his steed,
With an old woman fastened on before,
Who, tempted by some traitor's sordid greed,
   Letters in cipher to the British bore,
   Caught in the act as her boat left the shore.

Again, soon after Morgan's riflemen
Had joined the camp in white Virginia smocks,
Glover's marines chanced to be stationed then
In the next field, and snowballs hard as rocks
Flew fast and furious.　Washington, apprised,
Leapt from his saddle, vaulted o'er the fence,
Shook the ringleaders, frightened and surprised,
Stilled the disorder by his sterling sense;
   One from the Court, who saw the whole affair,
   Felt sure of freedom from what happened there.

Supplies delayed, and famine menacing,
Howe knew his danger and prepared retreat,
Till Percy woke to see, as came the spring,
Dorchester Heights, with Boston at its feet.
If left unharmed the town, allowed to go,
The British troops in sadness sail away,
And freedom smiles, and patriot hearts aglow,

One end achieved for which they hope and pray;
  And with them went three thousand refugees,
  Left land and home for exile and disease.

And toils had not made craven that hot blood
Which, since the Vikings, seethes within our veins,
Till, hot for strife, our angered sections stood
Opposed in civil war, — our country stains.
Not mine to tell the glory or the shame,
The fierce encounter or the deadly fight;
Both North and South with like assurance claim
Their foes were wrong, themselves were in the
        right;
  When numbers conquered, both alike content
  To their brave dead reared many a monument.

Here on the Charles the clustered arsenals
Stretching for many a rood along the mead,
Preserve the relics of the strife befalls
All nations justly proud of doughty deed;
Although the faith as Christians we profess
Teaches forbearance, and our passions check,
Let danger menace, wrong demand redress,
Its sacred lessons we but little reck,
  And rush to battle as we throng to feast, —
  On both alike crave blessing from the priest.

And yet to us the holy crucifix
Some other meaning was designed to tell;
When grievous wrong our fellow-men afflicts,
Or hostile nations threat, our own rebel,
What nobler than like Him our blood to shed,
If needed, to protect the heart or home;
To join our country's throng of martyred dead,
Nor fear, nor care, how glorious death may come?
   Surely no whispering monitor within
   Can stigmatize such sacrifice as sin.

CANTO XI.

HOMES OF THE POETS.

ITS halls and windows opening on the turf,
   Here stands an ancient mansion, lofty, grand,
Reared by a learned judge, a monarch serf
Before the blood of freemen freed the land:
Here Gerry dwelt, in loftiest station died,
Then of historic line a pastor pure,
Whose father's words the bondsmen's cords untied;
His gifted sons through ages will endure,
   And wisdom, wit, in Russell Lowell's lays,
   Keep ever bright and fresh his well-earned
      bays.

Begirt with groves where once the timid fawn
Ranged with her dam amid the tangled shade;
Bedecked with lofty elms, a spacious lawn
No limit to the spellbound eye betrayed;
Here all the country birds of sweetest note
Haunt the safe coverts, load the air with song,

Hawthorn and lilac all their fragrance float, —
Each flower in season all the summer long.
  Where richer pasture for a poet's soul,
  The poet's eye in finer frenzy roll?

Mountains may soar and boundless oceans spread,
And battlefields historic in their pride;
The castled crags may monument the dead,
And crowded cities roll their turbid tide;
But to the mind with little left to learn,
Imagination needs no help from sight;
Heroic breasts with pristine ardor burn,
Statesman and sage spring vividly to light;
  And, thus possessed, his web the poet weaves,
  His inspiration but the rustling leaves.

Here when the summer moon the azure mounts,
Shimmering with silver sheen the clustered trees,
The whippoorwill its moaning tale recounts,
And honeyed locust loads the freshening breeze;
Though thrush nor turtle-dove the echoes wake,
To spirit rapt the influences flow
In cadenced note from every bush and brake;
In kindred mood the brooding fancies glow,
  Absorbing beauty from that sacred shrine
  No time can stale, no limit can confine.

Or now the sun is up, the spicy morn,
And all the birds are warbling from the boughs,
Steeped in the dews the roses hide their thorn,
And crowing roosters drowsy sleepers rouse;
Truths that have crystalled into gems in dreams
Come sparkling forth beneath the morning light,
Each hidden ray with richer lustre gleams,
Destined to make all coming time more bright, —
　　To shed their halo round the honored name
　　Of him who earned but never cared for fame.

In yonder nook, beneath the sacred sod,
The martyred slain in their long silence sleep;
Along these blooming arcades patriots trod,
Sowing the seeds our after ages reap;
On ancient panes proud names to memory dear,
Upon the walls Salvator's twilight gloom,
The pious pastors in their mirth austere,
And in the quiet of that book-lined room
　　With patient toil the gifted scholar wrought,
　　Till all his own the universe of thought.

Here was he born, here grew to be a man;
In yonder college he both learned and taught;
Ancestral streams in genial currents ran,
And shaped events with human freedom fraught.

Who share our faith, respect his varied worth;
Who speak our language, profit by his word;
Wise with his wisdom, gayer for his mirth,
With antlers broad, the proudest of the herd:
  What other nation, near the British throne,
  More fitly represented than our own?   .

Near by these halls, in lines majestic, rears
Washington's own quarters veiled with clump and
      grove,
Where, when war ended, Craigie dwelt for years;
Four steeds an empress' sires in splendor drove;
There bloomed exotics spite the winter's cold:
His ice unmelted spites the summer's heat;
He 'd reaped a horde of precious lands and gold,
From wounds and bruises saved us from defeat;
  There Everett and Walker wielded rod;
  No greater — here our graceful poet trod.

Once in the dusk, steed fastened at the gate,
I mounted up the stairs to Washington's own
      room,
Where then the poet dwelt in lonely state,
His rapt imagination flushed with early bloom;
A flask of Rhenish, greeting frank and free,

His cheery talk the sunset hour beguiled,
And as the gorgeous coloring wrapped each tree,
Poet and sun and stream in splendor smiled;
   Here fame and fortune came to crown his life —
   Here friends that loved him, work and child
      and wife.

One friend most dearly prized from early youth,
In kindness knit, in fond affection one,
His grandsire, type of honor and of truth,
His country's idol next to Washington;
Bound by the like transmitted ties to Greene,
Oft at the poet's hearth a welcome guest,
His courteous manners and his gracious mien
Inspired with confidence, and all pride represt;
   Who knew his verses, knew too well the man
   With aught of awe his gifted genius scan.

That stately door with lock of ancient brass
Of huge dimensions, glittering like gold,
Those spacious stairs where gentle lad and lass
Have skipped in frolic till they too grew old;
That old-time clock that on the landing ticks,
Still beating on, though his own pulses stilled, —
What spectral forms the fancy bold depicts
Ascend, descend, with living substance filled!

And other flight as dainty, hid from sight,
To broad verandas, lawns with verdure bright.

There, on the left, his liberal board displayed
To feed the hungry, brilliant souls delight;
While opposite, the open doors betrayed
The pillared recess, and the bindings bright
Of cherished tomes of every school and tongue,
Where midst their leaves the busy poet delves,
What prose relates, in polished stanzas sung,
Seeking for precious ore among the shelves,
   Which by his genius purified and wrought,
   Their light long hid reveals to modern thought.

In front, the room that knows no idle hour, —
If pen be still, the mind in musing rapt;
The pregnant seed develops to the flower,
The gay parterre with bloom and fragrance lapped;
Words come unbid, and glowing fancies flow
As if by magic from that crystal well,
Whose iris drops reflect all man can know,
And inspiration needs no toil to tell;
   What is most fitting falls into its place,
   Nor of the throes creating leaves a trace.

Across the hall in front the presence room
With wainscot carved and pretty pictures decked;

The Pepperell children,—unforeseen their doom,—
Copley's bright genius in their sport reflect;
The stately mantel there by Vassal placed,
The window-seats that look across the Charles,
Each lifted sash a lovely glimpse encased
Of waving tulips, oaks the tempest gnarls;
   Surely no tripod from its sacred shrine
   So well could stir the soul to thoughts divine.

Between his home and where the river glides,
In time will loving hearts memorial rear
To one whose works while English speech abides
To all that speak it must be justly dear.
So long as pious souls in Nature find
The charm his lines so glowingly portray,
And Nature inspiration lends to mind,
His generous gift their grateful hearts repay;
   Upon the poet's walk their feet will stroll,
   His noble lines still penetrate the soul.

Oft mouldering mansions to base use return,
Their memory, as our own, obscured or lost;
Such as the Vassals built might surely earn
Fame more abiding, both from taste and cost.
Their ships saved England from the Armada's
     pride;

Leonard's home in Quincy still elicits praise,
And worth and wealth beneath its roof reside,
If where he died the rush of trade betrays.
 London's bright halls remain at Kensington,
 Where, amidst gems, his brilliant cousin shone.

Here sons and daughters, kindred side by side,
In fond affection dwelt and lettered ease;
Their placid days in wise contentment glide,
With flattering hope such days may never cease;
William, the youngest, gazed across the green
Where Harvard reared her walls of dusky red;
But long before stern war disturbed the scene
He reared in town a statelier home instead;
 There strove in vain to calm the growing hate,
 Ending for him but in the exile's fate.

About this Cambridge green, so long his home,
His numerous friends and kinsfolk clustered there,
And other honored shades at times have come,
Whose phantom forms still haunt the ambient air.
God's Acre to the right, with shattered stones,
Tells who of them once worked in glowing life;
There, stretched in peaceful rest, their mouldering
  bones,
At war perchance on earth, in hostile strife.

Christ Church lifts up, near by, her holy shrine,
Where they together shared the bread and
wine.

Students that haste at dawn to drowsy prayers
May deem this open space but dull and drear;
For him with thoughtful step and soul repairs
To grateful tasks, what precious memories cheer!
Beneath yon elm our nation's flag unfurled
When our great Chief for freedom drew the sword,
Not for his country only, but the world, —
Rose up a generous race with one accord,
To claim their rights, by brother men denied,
The rule of kings and foreign sway defied.

The church on one side, opposite the inn
By which the red lion flaunts his tawny tail,
Where learned professors thought it no great sin
To moisten tired lips with generous ale;
Still stands the house where steward and his son
On hungry stomachs fed the hungry mind,
Where sat those well-known chiefs, with Wash-
ington,
Guests of the noble Ward, his post resigned.
Tradition hallows still that festal board,
Its stirring speeches, martial songs, record.

And yonder group, veiled in the morning haze,
Heroes that struck the fetter from the slave,
Who can, unmoved, upon their record gaze, —
Ended such thraldom, helped their country save?
Or on that pile majestic, not remote,
Commemorates the sons whom Harvard gave,
Content their youth's best promises devote,
What most appalled in war, undaunted, brave,
    To keep that freedom which their fathers won,
    By lives well lost, by gallant deeds well done?

A generation passed since freedom bought,
The steward's house the pastor's manse became;
Holmes wrote his annals there, his sermons wrought,
And when he slept, there dwelt his race and name;
The natal place of his illustrious son,
Who there was nurtured, planted there his bays,
Whose various gifts have frequent laurels won
In science, brilliant prose, and magic lays;
    Lest when decayed, by stranger use defiled,
    Fair Harvard's now — the cradle of her child.

Later, harsh words gave place to hostile deed,
Embittered sections stood in stern array;
With earnest wish the bondsmen should be freed,
Hearts generous grew impatient of delay.

The poet gave his first-born to the cause,
His burning lines, more than battalions, told;
His genial soul cared less for man's applause
Than what was just and honest to uphold;
  As ancient bard inspired the hall and bower,
  His verse his country in its darkest hour.

CANTO XII.

HARVARD COLLEGE.

ALL honor to the hands that raised
This noble semblance to John Harvard's fame;
His eyes prophetic to the westward gaze,
Wherever learning glorifies his name;
Off where the sun beyond the western coast
Sinks in the sea, reflects in heaven above
His own pure spirit, that wide-spreading host
Owe all makes life worth living to his love.
Gaze back with grateful hearts that light to him
No time may dull or kindred stars can dim.

Steeped in the lore himself Emmanuel taught,
He came with staff and shell a pilgrim here,
And all unconscious of the good he wrought,
Other Emmanuels the desert cheer;
His fading strength left little hope to do
Much for his kind, before his fragile form
Released his gentle soul, that upward flew
To join the throng innumerable that swarm

8

To greet their elder brother, saint and sage,
Whose light more lustrous grows with every
    age.

Thus runs the Charles. Near by, upon its shore
Another river floweth, full and strong,
Gathering in force and volume, more and more,
All knowledge, wisdom, that to mind belong;
Facts proved, and principles, and Nature's laws
Working more clear, less turbid than before,
It traces purpose to the first great cause,
Interprets sensibly transmitted lore;
    What wrong or false, whatever just or right,
    Floods with the radiance of its new-born light.

Upon its library shelves, in order ranged,
Heap up deposits from the ages past,
Their fallacies by reason's touchstone changed,
By wash and wear — their theories recast.
Each generation, flushing in its strength,
Removes some quicksand, chafes some barrier
       through,
Till from its worn-out fetters freed at length
Its bosom heaves beneath a cloudless blue,
    Basks in the sunbeams of intelligence,
    And what was science, now is common-sense.

This not the place, nor mine the muse to sing
Our venerable Alma Mater's well-won praise;
To her proud gates the generations bring,
For her to teach, the noblest sons they raise.
If Massachusetts in the ages past
For useful culture has an honored name,
Distinguished authors but by few surpassed,
Much of her brightest inspiration came
 From Harvard's nurture of her generous youth
 In her own chosen motto, Christ and Truth.

What honored shades comprise the long-drawn
  scroll
Have swayed the sceptre of this favored realm!
Dunster and Chauncy head th' illustrious roll;
Oakes, Hoar, and Rogers followed at the helm;
Mather and Willard the first century close;
Then Leverett, Wadsworth, Holyoke, and Locke,
Langdon and Willard, as another flows;
Then Webber, Kirkland, Quincy feed their flock;
 To Everett, Sparks, and Walker passed along,
 Felton and Eliot end the illustrious throng.

Here master minds impelled by mutual zeal
Their finny tribes guide through its crystal caves,
Fathom its depths, to eager souls reveal

What stirs to effort, or from error saves;
In that famed stream of Lydia of old
That cleansed King Midas from his senseless lust,
He left behind him particles of gold
No time can waste, no baser dross can rust;
 In Harvard's genial currents those that dip,
 Make the world wiser for their pen and lip.

Who trod with Agassiz the mountain's crest,
Or dropped the plummet miles beneath the sea,
With Gray beheld the spring in blossom drest,
With Cooke the marvels weird of chemistry,
The starry universe with Pickering scan,
The planets weigh, or time their wondrous speed,
With Bowen mark the intellectual man,
With Lovering the inspired classics read, —
 Whatever paths be theirs in life's career,
 Who but are happier for what taught them here?

Is not the mind magnetic, where a throng
Of souls alert are busily employed,
Zealous, absorbed, press emulous along,
Value aright the privilege enjoyed;
Their fervor shared by all that dwell near by,
Resistless drawn within the magic spell,
Yield to the charm they seek in vain to fly,

Glad to partake, the enchanted circle swell?
   Thus at all times, about these sacred halls,
   Cluster in age, whose youth this spell recalls.

What crowds of teeming memories
Cling to these walls, indelible remain,
Of scholars lingering long beneath its trees
In sport or study honors high to gain!
Here knit the ties no lapse of time can chill,
In merry clubs exuberant with wit,
With classmates more sedate, remembered still,
Demure about its crowded benches sit;
   Finding too oft, although to study fain,
   In such companionship all efforts vain.

Were all their moments wasted?   Dullest clod
Grew animate beside its crystal course;
How many that its flowery margins trod
Quaffed life and vigor from its tireless source!
Though years had furrowed deep the thoughtful
      brow
Of Hedge and Farrar, Channing, Popkin, Ware,
Others as careworn, all forgotten now,
Yet master spirits, fashioned by that care,
   Adorned the land and State with laurel crown,
   Repaid her nurture by their just renown.

Not all distinguished; some too sensitive
For their full share of stimulating sport,
Rapt in their books, that often pleasure give
Complete as aught in ruder pastimes sought,
Off from the printed page their restless gaze
Fastens upon the azure arch above,
Or, fitful, ranges o'er the tangled maze
Of sunny meadows, crest, or quivering grove;
    What fond imaginings whiled the hours away
    Were better spent in study or at play!

In boyhood's days such visionary souls
In such enchantments dreamily afloat,
The fervid fancy through Elysium rolls,
Gloating on all that Scott or Byron wrote;
Roaming with Wordsworth over hill and glen,
With Wilson stalk the sea a living thing,
With Madoc fight his battles o'er again,
With Coleridge sweep with wizard-touch the string,
    Medea, Œdipus, dissolves in tears,
    While Irving's gentle genius thrills and cheers.

Two years beside Jamaica's fairy lake,
Four where Connecticut's swift currents flow,
Midst scenes of beauty kindred phantoms wake,
'T was mine to learn whatever good to know;

Not books alone, but Nature helped to yield
Its nutriment for faculty and thought,
Through all the seasons wandering far afield,
Joys the more precious that they were not bought;
　　Now in the saddle speeding through the wood,
　　Now floating down the stream in idle mood.

Later with Emerson, maturer grown,
A brilliant scholar in a gifted class,
Stackpole, with all accomplishments his own,
In taste and knowledge whom but few surpass;
From dawn to latest night my hungry mind,
While such instructors fashion, guide, inspire,
In classics, sciences, new meanings find,
Worked with a will no toil could ever tire, —
　　There in my study looking 'cross the stream,
　　With mind divided betwixt thought and dream.

Of problems wearied, or philosophy
Less luminous because a cheerless task,
Shaking our faculties and members free,
Exchanged the lesson for the foil and mask,
With one so late had passed himself the goal,
Much learned by rote, yet all well understood,
His pupil soon inscribed on Harvard roll,
One study overlooked to be made good, —

" Butler's Analogy," no easy stent,
Yet fairly mastered ere the week was spent.

Porceltians, Medfacs, opened wide their door,
The chocolate overboiled to many a jest,
In sword and sash the college flag I bore,
My chance companions ever of the best;
Such gayeties, for one of fragile frame,
Menaced consumption in a form to dread;
As to its final close the last term came,
The famed physician bade me leave my bed,
    And with good friends, about to cross the sea,
    In other climes escape such jeopardy.

Not in these pages seems it meet to tell
What may concern myself but not our stream;
Yet what in other lands my lot befell
Has interest enough such fault redeem.
'T is this that prompts my hesitating pen
Relate my happy chance to see and know
Many among the memorable men
Whose fame with every age must brighter grow:
    With whom a Harvard student sat at meat,
    Heard their own lips their inspired words repeat.

For hours at Greta Hall, at Southey's board,
Drinking in wisdom with our cups of tea,

Listening delighted to his boundless hoard
More than would seem in any mind could be;
A younger Coleridge, from Cambridge there,
Told me what tasks his college course comprised;
Yet when with that we Harvard here compare,
How much the same, both equally surprised:
Perhaps their system riper scholars grows,
As ours much less mature their studies close.

One happy summer day at Rydal Mount,
With William Hamilton, the poet's guest,
Hearing his wife in simple phrase recount
A death-bed scene just ended in its rest.
In regions so remote the pillow cheer
Of sick or dying, then a pious rite,
Her turn had come to watch a dalesman near,
Who lingering conscious through the night,
His anguished spirit every deed recalled,
In that dread hour his cankered soul appalled.

But cheerier converse the swift hours beguiled
As various topics well in turn discussed;
The noon long past when in a cavern wild
Lodore upon our spellbound vision burst;
Then roaming round about each favorite haunt,
A swivel, hid near by, the stillness broke, —

The hills reverberate the dying chant,
As each, in turn, to sound so loud awoke;
   The sun, declining, purpled wood and lake
   As to the poet's house our way we take.

France, resolute to set her people free
From kings who did not for their subjects reign,
Drove out their hapless Charles beyond the sea,
Heaped up the Paris streets with Frenchmen slain;
In wild commotion, frenzied, tempest-tossed,
Her gates against both friend and foeman closed,
A friend with me who had the ocean crossed,
To Scotland's shrines a pilgrimage proposed;
   How oft at home we hearkened with delight
   To his rich flow of thought and converse bright!

In art and letters versed, the chosen friend
Of gifted men whose fame can never fade,
With pious steps we first to Cambridge wend,
To hall and colleges our homage paid;
To our own Cambridge both allegiance own, —
One as a pupil, he as ruling sage.
Of our own founder, Harvard, little known,
More to discover, first our thoughts engage;
   Exile and our harsh climate broke his health:
   Our college and his widow shared his wealth.

To Waters then, delving in records old,
Who teaches worth 's to no degree confined,
That those who wove or tilled, who bought or sold,
Transmit their nobler nature to their kind;
Born by the Thames where trade floats up and down,
Its healthy pulses with the century beat,
Without his seeking came to him renown
Circling the spacious earth with busy feet.
    And sure no pyramid or historic page
    A nobler monument from age to age.

Age then, with pious word and open palm,
Invoked God's blessing on the youthful brow;
Before another month upon my head,
Scotland's great wizard, as then, vivid now,
Near midnight, as to Melrose we passed on,
Standing at Abbotsford on his portal there,
Bestowed on parting guest his benison, —
" God bless you, my dear boy! " his loving prayer.
    Even Southey, though in manner more reserved,
    In benediction the like form observed.

At Liston Place, beneath the stately trees
Our aged host had from our forests brought,
When he the first to represent the Crown
Here, where for freedom not in vain was fought;

His father's farm-house to a castle grown,
There Mrs. Hemans his most favored guest,
Already in both lands her genius known,
Her " Pilgrim Fathers " in our farthest west;
   That summer morn, as by her side we strolled,
   On wings of gossamer the hours rolled.

Well up the hill stood, on a level lawn,
In simple grace, the mansion of the seer,
Whose windows greet the coming of the dawn,
Embrace the mountain grandeur far and near;
With ivy draped, within, books everywhere,
A fitting home for Nature's child to dwell,
His silver locks stream in the summer air,
As on his portal slab we bade farewell;
   That gentle hand in gentle kindness pressed
   Upon my brow, as he in parting blessed.

Still borne in mind that dawn of summer-tide,
With Gray and Gregory aroused from bed,
From Edinburgh we paced with quickened stride
To Craigcrook Castle, where its breakfast spread;
In cosey nook within its rounded tower,
Midst fragrant roses we enchanted sit;
The child and wife in their enchanting bower,
The sparkling Jeffries bubbling o'er with wit;

His buxom lassie bordering on sixteen —
My seat, as stranger, sire and child between.

Fresh from her couch, all garbed in vestal white,
Her bird of golden plumage on her arm,
Ribbons afloat with tints of golden light,
Graceful and blooming, with each spell to charm, —
In heaven and earth no moment more complete
Than such a morn in such companionship;
With cheeriest spirits we contented meet,
And wit and eloquence inspire the lip;
    Near fifty years, since that most blessed day,
    In strange vicissitudes have sped away.

Well I recall how Pollok's " Course of Time,"
Not long before, the admiring world bewitched,
Which to our simple taste seemed quite sublime, —
We ventured to declare Young's verse enriched;
The king of critics, quick to mark amiss
Where these dark poets differed, not agreed,
With his bright sallies of antithesis,
And brilliant contrasts his rich fancies breed,
    Pronounced " Night Thoughts" the wittiest of
        verse,
    Ideas translucent and expressions terse.

With flights of fancy ended our repast;
Our host then led us to the vale below,—
Gardens and trellis in profusion passed,
And lofty trees of his own planting grow;
We strolled, and hearkened to this mental feast
Sparkling and rippling, with no shade of gloom;
The flow of mirth and fancy never ceased
Till we our path to Edinburgh resume,
  Pleased to have clasped in friendly grip the
     hand
  Of him as critic known in every land.

Farewell, fair Harvard! when we count the debt
The country owes to lessons thou hast taught,
Justice and truth and wisdom, — how forget
Thy sons in life's hard struggle well have fought?
How their example, their achievements, due
To precepts that thy loving care instils,
The generations to thy teachings true,
The object of existence each fulfils,
  In brighter lustre shall thy glory shine;
  Each child thou nurturest be more divine.

CANTO XIII.

MOUNT AUBURN.

HERE upon my sofa, fire burning low,
　　Midst the murky shadows ghostly forms ap-
　　　　pear,
Fancies fond and fleeting, visions come and go,
Now bright and cheerful, now sad and drear;
I remember when a student in yonder college halls
Near by the woods primeval, dense with bush and
　　　　brake,
All around extending dilapidated walls,
Hoary oaks and beeches that in mystic whispers
　　　　spake;
　Where lichen-mantled bowlders piled gray amid
　　　　the trees,
　In solemn grandeur waving their branches in the
　　　　breeze.

If haunted by the Wicked One, as the story went,
He displayed his taste in choosing such congenial
　　　　haunt,

Deep in the rocks his hoofs had left their dent,
Students in the twilight had met him grim and
　　gaunt;
It is said of one great genius, that by the lightning's
　　flash
His dark majestic visage did uncanny seem,
Perhaps some embryo statesman, startled mid the
　　crash,
Beheld his own reflected in some ambitious dream;
　For every Alma Mater numbers many a son
　That soars among the heroes before his race
　　begun.

And oft the pallid scholar, prone to ponder and to
　　muse,
Strolled among these tangles, suggestive more than
　　books,
Random cogitations from hidden fountains ooze,
And from tiny trickles sparkle into brooks.
They called the place Sweet Auburn, deserted and
　　forlorn;
But no ancient village had there mouldered into
　　dust,
Or since the Indians left it Christian child been
　　born, —
It was a simple wood-lot of forest kings august;

Belonging with the farmstead to race of sturdy
　　carles,
Whose home for generations looked down upon
　　the Charles.

In one quiet corner, when their work was done,
They gathered to their fathers in one common tomb,
Sleeping by the river where their course begun,
With their loving kinsfolk to wait the final doom,—
One that they feared not, for simple were their
　　lives;
They earned their bread with labor, were honest
　　and devout,
Nurturing well their children, thoughtful of their
　　wives,
Filial to their parents whose sands were ebbing out:
　Guests were kindly welcomed, and no honest
　　poor
Went out cold or hungry from their ample store.

All throughout New England, on some shaded hill,
Or where gleaming rivers down to ocean glide,
Such little graveyards rows of tombstones fill,
And groups of loving kindred slumber side by side;
Seasons come and pass, flowers and emerald turf,
Winter's spotless mantle for their winding-sheet,

9

Tempests or the zephyr, or the rolling surf,
Their ceaseless requiem about their ashes beat;
 Whilst their blessèd spirits in unending bliss
 Hark to strains ecstatic in happier realms than this.

Before earth's many marvels to science stood re-
  vealed,
All its glowing splendors, its boundless realms of
  space,
Its laws and purpose from all but God concealed,
Man thought it but created for his own dwelling-
  place;
But as the field of knowledge opened wider to his
  view,
He recognized our planet among the least of all;
He became more humble as he wiser grew,
And as from his dazed vision the scales of darkness
  fall,
 He learns how far more glorious the divine
  Creator's will
 Than that vast world of matter his purposes fulfil.

Perhaps a growing feeling that these forms of clay
Are but veils, concealing from our eyes the light,
That on their dissolution dawns more perfect day,
It is that makes them of less value in our sight;
All the spicy cerements of embalmèd kings,

Their ponderous sepulchres that heavy lade the
    earth,
Tomb within the churches, that to the pious brings
Solace mid the shadows of the second birth,
    Yield to the faith that He who died to save,
    Will find his followers in the humblest grave.

Possibly the verse upon the marble stones
Shakspeare indited for his Stratford tomb —
" Cursed be the mortal that removes these bones "—
Shadows the rest, robs death of half its gloom;
And who at summer evening, when the church's
    bell
Tolls out the knell of some departing soul,
In that loveliest chapel, which he loved so well,
Beside the river whose waters murmuring roll,
    But desires for himself like undisturbed repose
    So long as water runs, or fragrant violet grows?

We have our ancient churchyards, filled with dust
Of saints and heroes, faithful, if austere,
Commingled now in heaven with the good and just,
Made perfect through the love that knows no fear;
Who that has read the annals of our past
Till those long dead breathe, walk, and speak
    again,

But must recall that current, free and fast,
Of lovely women and of noble men,
  In quick succession left the busy street
  To rest beneath the sod their weary feet?

That chapel ground where sleep our patriarch sires,
Granary that garnered many a patriot saint,
Amidst whose ashes glow their wonted fires
To keep in heart the living souls that faint;
Illustrious fathers dauntless heroes bred,
Jurists and statesmen, who in days of old,
In strife for freedom, in the peril led,
Of fearless spirit and heroic mould,
  With many a mother whose whispers from below
  Plainly teach their children the paths that they
    should go.

Yet as great cities in their wealth expand,
Fashion and traffic needing all the space,
Succeeding generations can no more command
For friends they mourn a fitting burial-place;
It was a happy foresight that in time secured
This lovely region for their loved and lost,
Where Nature's growth, by centuries matured,
Outliving monuments of art and cost,
  Divests the tomb of all that's dull or sad,
  Shrouded in snow, or by the summer clad.

Of all conditions, every age, the throng
Pace with their throbbing hearts their footsteps
    keep;
For peace and rest from all their sorrows long,
Yet dread the horrors of the dreamless sleep;
Some with unfaltering faith approach the tomb,
Confiding in the love they trusted here;
Whilst guilty consciences confront their doom
Appalled, and shuddering at the judgment near;
  But whether loath to go or glad to stay,
  Resistless fate drives all alike away.

In loneliness and sorrow, in poverty or pain,
Memory a rankle, not a hope but gone,
Knowing that affection can never bless again
To keep their hearts from aching, cheer their souls
    forlorn,   ·
Their nights a restless vigil, their days a weary
    round,
Shut out from every solace, without faith in prayer,
How many yearn to lay their bodies in the ground,
And for resurrection have no wish or care!
  Glad if life be ended, and no consciousness come
    back
  Of torments they have suffered while here upon
    its rack.

When we remember the friends, all linked together,
Who from pleasant windows gazed out upon the
    groves
Of elm and ash and linden in the summer weather,
Where over leaves and waters the eye delighted
    roves;
Or when in winter's midnight the frosty stars were
    twinkling,
The lovely maids and gallants with fond affection
    glow,
To the lute and viol, the harps melodious tinkling,
As of love and friendship kind expressions flow, —
  Sad such grateful measures should ever end in
      gloom,
  And one and then another rest in the silent
      tomb!

Here midst their inspiration came the poets and
    the sages,
Orators conning speeches to charm the ears of
    men,
Historians, their pages enriched with lore of ages,
For their country's welfare those who plied the pen;
Lucid minds, like Bowditch, in the balance weighing
Every orb that courses to the verge of space;
Or the saintly Channing, with spirit's eye surveying

Paths to lead to heaven a degenerate race:
  Their once familiar presence long vanished from
    the sight,
  Though from the works they left us can never
    fade the light.

The sorrowing nations, 'neath this sacred sward
Mourn Agassiz, who here his country chose,
In search of truth the ocean depths explored,
Counted the ages midst the Alpine snows;
Nature to him displayed her sibyl leaves
Till all organic swarmed again to view,
Knowledge with science into wisdom weaves,
As times long past their mysteries renew;
  At last, familiar with sublimer spheres,
  To him unveiled the universe appears.

Of that Parian marble Praxiteles charmed to life,
His golden voices breathing richest pearls of
    thought,
Every movement graceful, emotions quick and rife
Waking into music as his quickening genius
    wrought;
Imagination teeming, by chastened taste restrained,
With the widest culture, exquisite good sense,
His spirit thoughtful, tender, with dignity sustained

Heaven's inspiration in fervid eloquence.
  No more consummate orator could Athens boast,
    or Rome,
  Than Everett, who resteth here in his last earthly
    home.

Story, whom no labor wearied, many a theme ob-
    scure,
With boundless stores of learning, the keenest sense
    of right,
However dim or dreary, his sunshine spirit pure
Marshalled into order, flooded with its light.
None kinder or more genial when with his fellow-
    men,
To his sympathetic nature naught indifferent or dull ;
From exhaustless fountains, with tireless lip and pen,
His life flowed full and placid, knew no ebb or lull.
  Death to one so active brought neither dread
    nor gloom,
  As in these shades he planted he found his wel-
    come tomb.

Cushing, Parsons, Parker, elsewhere found their rest ;
Dana, with son and grandson, sleeps here beneath
    this sod ;
Shaw, who wore their ermine, peer among the best,

The just man made perfect walked hitherward with
　　God ;
No precedents misled him, no bias ever swerved,
No higher court o'erruled him, no aspirations swayed,
No adverse decision pretended undeserved,
Never course of justice by neglect delayed.
　Here lie the sacred ashes of one both good and
　　great,
　Who the day of his own judgment well may fear-
　　lessly await.

Choate, the Heaven-gifted, the Bayard of the law,
Of stately form, with eye of fire, or all abeam with love,
Tones thrilling with emotion, as their impassioned
　　soar
Lifted who heard, resistless, to kindred realms above.
Sure, no more brilliant genius or richer rush of words
E'er poured from heights of eloquence to dazzle or
　　persuade ;
Now lion-like majestic, now warbling with the birds,
As about the mighty torrent his flashing fancy
　　played.
　With dirges here we brought him, and with our
　　solemn tread
　Our swelling hearts in unison beat homage to
　　the dead.

Within yon shrine of marble, where the mantling
      ivy clings,
Winthrop and Adams, Otis, Channing, stand;
Declining day a warmer radiance flings, —
The dawn still finds unchanged the illustrious
      band.
While freedom, virtue, wisdom, still hold sway,
Mankind will ever keep their halo bright;
To worth like theirs its cheerful homage pay,
The historic page their glorious deeds recite.
    Yet all the laurels crown their proud career,
    Ashes and dust to higher hopes that cheer.

Not mine the record of that wondrous throng,
So many known while living, who now are honored
      dead;
Artists and poets who witched the world with song,
Priests and physicians who smoothed the dying bed.
Our merchant princes, whose wealth enriched the
      State,
Builders of our cities, turned their walls to
      stone,
Philanthropists, whose monuments their varied worth
      relate,
Or the admirable women that well their work had
      done.

These branches, as they rustle, whisper many a
    noble name,
For whom their lives have earned their imperish-
    able fame.

From mould like theirs, bedewed with sorrow's tears,
Plants numberless in rich luxuriance grow;
Each fragrant bloom its graceful petals rears,
Till nipped by frost they droop beneath the snow;
There sleep and rest till cometh back the spring,
The genial warmth revivifies from death;
From spray to spray the happy warblers sing,
The breezes fan them with enamoured breath;
    And when perfected in their earthly sod,
    Transplanted to the garden of their God.

From here below no eye may penetrate
That spirit world we hope to call our own;
That such exists, a consciousness innate
Gains strength from reason with the ages flown;
Yet if inscrutable the Will Divine,
Made in His image, we can well believe
Mercy and love must fashion the design,
Hopes planted in our souls will not deceive, —
    That when upon this life we close our eyes,
    Far brighter realms await beyond the skies.

This but suggests, the sacred Scriptures tell
In other ways, that death is but a stage;
Annihilation, human minds repel;
Experience, conscience, the historic page,
Design in Nature and design in man,
Pain, sorrow, sin, the cross ordained by love, —
All, forming part of one consistent plan,
Proclaim this life the seed of one above;
    And here beside the grave, the mouldering sod
    Reveals to man the purposes of God.

What heaven may be, by Providence concealed,
Faith can conjecture from experience here;
Those loved on earth again to us revealed,
Eager to greet our shadows hovering near,
What sacred joy, as they in glory clad
Throw wide the gates that we may enter in,
Who watched our course, when we were tempted,
       sad,
Helped us, perhaps, the victory to win!
    All we have known below, or come before,
    Happy we now have met to part no more.

Perchance all that innumerable race
Whose blood we shared, with whom in faith were
      one,

From Eden's mystic fall restored to grace,
Their pilgrimage on earth, of trial, done,
Now sing hosannas to their loving Lord,
Who all created, and who all directs, —
In psalm and hymn unite with one accord,
Each joyous soul His radiance reflects.
  Through all His many mansions near His throne,
  With grateful love adore who reigns alone.

And as with fond affection nestle round,
Cast off the bonds of flesh, the mind renewed,
By narrow paths it trod no longer bound,
Its eyes, unveiled, behold infinitude.
No past or future, — ever present spread
Creation vast to the enchanted sight;
Material worlds in rhythmic measures tread,
Shadow of substance, spirit world of light;
  Delight ineffable, all left to know
  Whose laws and marvels their wise purpose show.

How often by the coffin of a friend,
The wise and good, the generous and gay,
Whose intercourse will now no longer lend
Its cheer and solace to our lonelier way,
We feel assurance he 's but gone before, —
That one so free from guile, with every grace,

Again will greet us on that other shore;
Once more beheld that long familiar face,
  So late uplifted, lay on yonder mound
  With sorrowing kinsfolk clustering around.

Or flitting upwards to congenial skies,
Behind her left the dross that held her bound,
With angel guides her happy wings she plies,
Her seraph form with wreaths immortal crowned.
Of all the forms that living clay puts on,
Childhood and prime, and tresses white with age,
All that of each is loveliest blent in one,
As loved by old and young, as good as sage,
  She speeds aloft beyond the azure dome,
  And saints their sweetest sister welcome home.

Will all find welcome?   Room enough for all.
The spirit world has neither fence nor bound;
Mercies unstrained on good and evil fall,
The most depraved, with penitence is crowned.
Throughout the universe no place for hell,
Save in the guilty, tortured by remorse;
The festering conscience will its secrets tell,
Then find, at last, forgiveness in the cross, —
  If still remembered, every fault and sin
  Washed with its blood as they had never been.

Trial, temptation, God's kind providence,
Stand with their flaming swords at Heaven's gate
That none pass through not clothed in innocence;
Its folds unused would on their hinges grate.
By sorrow tried, still trusting in His love,
Tempted, still striving from the wrong t' abstain,
If yielding, prayed assistance from above,
Welcomed the cross if we His paths regain,
   Man struggles on and upward to the goal,
   Then, fearless, enters in, a ransomed soul.

That azure noonday how can man forget?
Kneeling despondent by that crowded way,
He sought the help to save, by sins beset,
And rose assured he should no longer stray.
Many the life thus saved from wretchedness,
For pitying Love hears every mortal prayer.
Nor His alone to pardon, but to bless;
His happy rest, with all His children share
   What path now flecked by Heaven's glimmer,
      shed
   To show the steps we may with safety tread.

Thus the proud race we claim to be our own
Live out their span, then moulder 'neath the sod;
Their souls still sentient pass to realms unknown,

With steadfast trust in their creating God.
Their life, transmitted, animates fresh forms,
Who in their turn spring up, mature, decay;
Enjoy life's blessings, strengthen with its storms,
Then in its sepulchres return to clay.
    The generations pass, the race still lives,
    Content to take what He in wisdom gives.

Still calmly flow the rivers, still shines the daily sun,
The tides impede their progress, the clouds obscure
        its ray;
They tell us time is fleeting, our course may not be
        run,
Yet we may die to-morrow, or we may die to-
        day.
Would that this task were finished, as also many
        more;
Not mine the time t' appoint, but may I ready
        be,
My house here put in order as I seek the other
        shore,
And there my cross admitting, may I there my
        Saviour see.
    Again upon the current I loose my little boat,
    For Charles has much to tell us as to the sea we
        float.

CANTO XIV.

ANNEX TO HARVARD COLLEGE.

PROUDLY upon the steps of Holworthy,
    Waved the gay banner of the Harvard corps,
Which, on its folds of silken blazonry,
The college arms, the State's, and nation's bore.
The skies were cloudless, and the stirring band
Awoke the echoes of the halls around,
Whose wrinkled fronts in pensive glamour stand,
Veiled by umbrageous trees that fleck the ground.
    That flag, then gorgeous which all eyes observe,
    Tattered, Porcellians sacredly preserve.

Our tasks as soldiers daintily discharged,
We marched along God's Acre, Appian Way,
To that grand mansion, recently enlarged,
Where maids uncloistered pass the livelong day;
Where they con Greek or cipher out a star.
A cordial welcome greets us — each his guest —
From that proud form and leader of the bar,
As then the mode, in rich apparel dressed.

Many among us to his friends well known;
Many whose sires he cherished as his own.

Within the rooms, the fairest of the fair,
The maid of frolic lip and laughing eye,
And buds and blossoms far beyond compare,
Brimming with mirth, not yet had learned to sigh;
The choicest flowers from all the gardens round
Exhaled their fragrance on the autumn breeze,
The lovely salvia, then less frequent found;
Whilst martial strains from underneath the trees
     Mingled their music with the gush of tone
     From happy hearts that knew but joy alone.

Nor these alone the memories recalled —
Beside me sits the daughter of our host,
Whose thrilling song our choicest souls enthralled;
Fair dames and noblest men, our social boast;
Nor be forgot that honored Admiral,
Whose science pulsed the universe of space,
Who prompt responded at his country's call,
In naval annals won a foremost place;
     Nor their sweet sister, by all saints impelled,
     In art the guide, in wisdom few excelled.

Beneath that roof my kinsmen, sire and son,
Lived many happy years of peace and love;

The father and the gifted wife passed on,
Sure of kind welcome in the realms above.
Here, too, her cultured parents came and went,
Models of all lent social life a charm,
On giving pleasure every thought intent,
In soothing sorrow every look its balm;
 What happiness such Christian souls enjoy!
 Its choicest blessings, oft, in its alloy.

Near by the gate still stands the lofty elm
Where Washington for freedom drew the sword,
Not as a conqueror, to gain a realm, —
His country's gratitude his sole reward;
No nobler words e'er sanctified a cause,
Or hearts more generous e'er imperilled life;
The event deserved and earned the world's ap-
  plause,
And its example disciplined for strife.
 The teeth by Cadmus sown grew armèd men,
 To break the fetters of his countrymen.

The sons of Harvard needed not to learn
The ways and methods of the fields of war;
Their land endangered, their bosoms burn
To meet the peril as it threats afar;
Their books cast down, they seize the sword and gun,

Rush to the front, and dauntless shed their blood;
For country die, when their brave course has
    run,
Nor care how perish, or by field or flood.
  If few came back, still, the dark bondmen free
  Assure to all their immortality.

But peace, too, has its laurels; thoughtful soul
May raze the fallacies from minds pervert,
The poor relieve, the sorrowing console,
The vicious and the infidel convert;
Who train the stupid, brighten up the dull,
And misery in all its forms make glad,
From their own plenty grapes and roses cull
To soothe the fever, or to cheer the sad.
  More glorious thus the tiresome hours to fill,
  Than on the field of battle wound or kill.

No task more worthy than to shape and mould
The callow maid to noblest womanhood,
The character in all its grace unfold,
The heart, to all that's sensitive and good;
Fill full the mind with all the varied lore
Reveals the universe, and Him, creates;
Enrich the memory with that precious store
To taste, and art, and human life relates;

Be still content, so ever long the span,
In fancy free, or peerless mate of man.

What fitter altar for creation's shrine
Than reared by him, of Nature hierarch,
Or hers whose steps along his life-path shine,
On sands of time their honored impress make?
With such exemplars, angel visitants
May well stoop down to sip the crystal spring,
Then soar aloft, the very stars entrance,
As betwixt heaven and earth they chorals sing;
Or up and on, as follows day the night,
Regain their home, the seraphim of light.

Had this been happiest, such no doubt their lot;
Scripture and reason tell the reasons why
These dazzling dreams for human beings, not
What was designed for earthly destiny.
Wisdom and virtue out of trouble grow;
Care, disappointment, serve as whip and spur,
Teaching the mind what it is best to know,
Keeping warm the heart, and its emotion stir;
Why, then, should any mortal soul repine
At ills assimilate to the divine?

Fauna and flora, similar, diverse,
Germ, grow, live out their periods assigned;

Our human race their several tasks rehearse,
Form part mysterious of the general mind;
The lowlier reptiles creep along the earth,
The fish and fowl swim through the sea and air;
Mankind alone, progressive from their birth,
With their Creator speech and wisdom share,
    Like sturdy oak, or like the willow frail,
    Bend to the breeze, or struggle with the gale.

If Adam earliest, and then gentle Eve,
In Eden dwelt, with nought but to obey,
She quick to learn and easy to deceive,
Thirsty for knowledge, led him first astray, —
If parable, it teaches more than truth,
A lesson all of us may take to heart,
That if we would escape the serpent's tooth,
We best leave Adam to his books apart;
    Nor let his weakness by a siren song
    Be blindly led from what is right to wrong.

Contrast, variety, the fertile source
Of life and love, and all that life holds dear;
Antagonism multiplies the force
That rends the rock, and draws the planets near;
Kept separate, its harmless vigor grows,
In self-absorption garners up its strength,

Until, mature, its heaped-up current flows,
And, swept away all obstacles at length,
   Spreads in luxuriance over field and fold,
   With ample harvests as the years are told.

When side by side the lamb and lion lay,
No hostile nations shed fraternal blood,
No selfish yearnings innocence betray,
Or later guilt provoke another flood;
When all of us the self-same pages read,
With pulse as calm as throbs in marble vein;
When we are tempted, no monition need,
Shrink from no shadow, lest it leave a stain, —
   One *Alma Mater* will for all suffice,
   And thus regained our long-lost paradise.

Nor far to seek. Beside yon purple beech
Nuthall and Gray spread wide their floral realm,
To kindred tastes the laws of Nature teach, —
How creeps the vine, or soars the lofty elm,
In vast variety of tints and scents,
An endless loveliness of graceful form;
Through the arched vistas, 'mid the thickets dense,
The birds and bees with song melodious swarm;
   And every sense, each with its special zest,
   Luxuriates in what it loves the best.

All round the earth the climes and seasons wind
The growth best fitted to adorn and cheer;
In wreaths of beauty souls congenial bind,
And sympathies draw loving natures near;
In tangled mazes of supreme delight,
The heart, the grape, with luscious flavor fill,
Ripen their juices in the warmth and light,
From rose and violet their sweets distil;
    Garden and orchard, and the teeming field,
    To each and all their grateful harvest yield.

Emblems of innocence by faith restored,
Lost Eden that Gethsemane redeems,
The Great Supreme in all his works adored,
His universe with love and mercy teem;
He clothes the lily — with its simple grace
Not Solomon in all his glory vies;
Throughout the ages we His wisdom trace,
His daily providence with pleased surprise;
    His gift most precious, still the guiltless soul
    Kept pure from dross by His benign control.

How oft we gathered of a Sabbath eve —
Our kindly hostess one we loved so well
We lingered long, and, ever loath to leave,
Outwatched the stars as they in ocean fell;

Beneath the trees, or where the jutting roof
Hangs down with vines, or honeysuckles cling
In fragrant meshes, dangling, warp and woof
Blend in the moonlight, as the thrushes' song,
  Their hush and ripple mingled in their notes,
  As up the sky their quiet music floats.

As waning moons denote the horoscope,
A year has sped since three loved classmates came,
With eager footsteps climbed the graceful slope,
Pleased to recall each shrub we knew by name;
The sun was setting, and the shades of night
Fell darkling down upon the bosks and bowers,
The western sky all full of lurid light,
As pattering rain-drops turned to drenching showers.
  But soon, the shelter of the house regained,
  The star-lit scene without a cloud remained.

BOSTON.

STILL rolling down the river, still sweeping up
    its tide,
Their contending currents mingle in the bay
Which, when our century opened, extended far
    and wide,
From the bridge of Craigie to where the rope-walk
    lay, —
Up to the Common flagstaff, away to Corey's hill,
Spring floods, two fathom above their lowest ebb,
Brought the purest water and the freshest breeze;
Their many channels in their tangled web,
Health and vigor from out the briny seas;
    Gleaming in the sunshine, or lurid in the storm,
    As clouds that hovered over assumed each
    changing form.

On profit bent, trade crowded on the shore;
The builders-up of cities, grown in pride,
Heed little what Canute taught long before,
That kings themselves can stay nor time nor tide;

Yet still they rashly bridled up the sea,
Wielding heavy iron, grinding out the grain,
Marring splendid basins, and yet lived to see
The boldest against Nature ever work in vain;
    The wash that flushed our channels, built for us
        our trade,
    Grown shoal and silted, — Boston was betrayed.

And yet still held in honor, their names are not
       forgot,
All around us relics of their taste and skill,
In clustered homes, deck many a desert spot;
Traffic and commerce levelling bog and hill,
Heights towering upwards from the harbor's brink.
The rock and clay they cast into the sea,
As valleys rise and rugged hillocks sink;
Pasture and field of mingling turf and tree
    Give place to lofty blocks for house or trade,
    And man usurps the Edens Nature made.

While thus upon the shore this havoc wrought
Despoiled the garden, groves primeval felled,
The frolic Charles, emerging, vainly sought
The wide-spread waters, once its basins held;
For public spirit or that private greed
Turned creek or forest into street or mart,

To mischief caused gave little thought or heed,
Where they of fame or profit crave their part,
    Though our fair port, that Providence designed
    For a great city, became lost to mind.

Across to Muddy Brook, three miles away,
A dam divides in two the tidal space;
Another intersects this pent-up bay, —
For use contrived, yet not devoid of grace;
The basin next the hill receives the tide,
As daily, twice, its floods creep from the deep;
Then through the flumes its heaped-up currents
       glide,
Force through the opening gates, to ocean sweep;
    Sanguine the hope, the disappointment sore —
    Flumes, wheels, and belts have ceased forever-
    more.

Where once these works, long lines of stately homes
Now rear their fronts of every form and hue;
From far away discerning affluence comes
To share delights both ever fresh and new;
Music, and art, and social intercourse,
The drama, concert, pulpit, and the chance
Of hearing gifted minds in wise discourse,
The rink, the ride, or, if still young, the dance;

The blest rewards of innocence and health,
If just and generous, give chief worth to wealth.

Outside, the proud array of palaces
Looks out upon what's left us of the bay,
The straitened river, vexed and ill at ease,
Labors and frets along its devious way;
The rails below that crowd its lessening span,
Choke with their slime, obstruct with their support;
Experts, for pay, delude the simple man, —
If not too honest, by base lucre bought.
    What benefit from all the railroads cost,
    If cars run empty to a harbor lost?

Go scan the map, and learn the reasons why
Thronged seaports thrive, and help enrich the
        State.
Some river broad and deep runs rushing by,
Or lesser streams their valleys wide dilate
Above the shores where commerce loves to dwell.
Drink in the restless sea whose daily scour
The tide and streams to heavy volume swell;
Thus swept the channels by their mighty power
    Unchanged as Nature formed, the heaviest
        craft
    Into safe harbors steam and breezes waft.

For prospered city, for its people's pride,
Where, 'long the coast, found harbors more com-
   plete
Than Winthrop chose, with Providence to guide,
For pious souls that crowd his wearied fleet?
From fair Nahant to far-off Alderton,
Ten miles or more, its area westward spread,
Its emerald islands, gleaming in the sun,
Leaving strait channels that to anchorage led,
 Sheltering its roadsteads for whole fleets to moor,
 Guarding as sentinels its ocean door.

Once clothed with trees, now swept by tempest
   bare,
Poverty found shelter, vice its prison drear;,
With balm of healing, the salubrious air
Soothes the festered conscience, of misery dries
   the tear;
On the restless waters vessels come and go, —
Yachts and stately steamers, barks of low degree,
On quests of trade or pleasure, gliding to and fro,
Whether summer skies be smiling, or dark the
   boisterous sea.
 While with precaution brave men approaches
   guard,
 No fear of hostile cruisers to frighten or bombard.

By kindly fortune favored, taste and culture blessed,
All round the globe our sons and daughters roam;
Still pride of their own country warms their breast,
Their public spirit yearns to bless their home;
No place so poor but those that dwell there love;
Such, everywhere, the universal plan, —
We fondly cling where placed by power above,
And dearly prize our heritage as man;
 Far we may wander o'er this spacious earth,
 Still longing for the spot that gave us birth.

Here from its cradle, still its fair renown
Girdles the orb, resounds through every age,
From golden dome, its loftiest summit's crown,
To where the distant ocean spends its rage;
We dearly cherish this our natal place,
And scorn the greed that would its glory mar,
Venality that can its name disgrace,
Averting perils threatening from afar.
 God grant our wisdom may our port defend,
 On which its safety and our hopes depend!

And not our port alone. Men true and good
Through all the past intrusted with affairs;
To their good sense, unswerving rectitude,
We owe a rule that with the best compares.

Must this be changed?   Oh, vile and abject crew
Unseemly scramble after place and power, —
Not for aught good they can the public do,
But what the industrious earn they may devour!
   The ignorant and vicious they mislead,
   To feed their vanity or sate their greed.

No State so firm or stable but decays
With vile corruption gnawing at its base.
The Providential plan in varied ways
Bestows its choicest blessings on that race
Who sensibly accept its obvious laws,
With grateful hearts requite its kindly care;
Who, when by evil tempted, instant pause;
Honest and scrupulous, undoubting, dare
   To recognize that precept as divine, —
   Rests good and evil upon " mine and thine."

Conscience, if unenlightened, often swerves
Unless in youth such principles instilled;
That nation well the consequence deserves
That leaves this sacred duty unfulfilled.
In vain, content on other base to build;
All progress for mankind must ever rest —
That he shall reap who has the harvest tilled.
Who reaps and saves, more frugal than the rest,

Or by his prudent foresight heaps his store,
May spend or keep his own for evermore.

If all were Christians, with one faith and trust,
No crafty dogmas simple minds disturbed,
No pride of domineering bred disgust,
The Sermon on the Mount each passion curbed;
If, in humility like His, we strove
For others' happiness and not our own,
Our prayers as fervid as when in the grove
His intercessions reached His father's throne, —
  Though with sorrow laden, we should bear the
    cross,
  Though our hearts were troubled, little be the
    loss.

Not ours to know His purpose or His plan.
Born into life on earth, our sense and lot,
Our own experience, but few lustres span;
We disappear, — that we have lived, forgot.
But history, science, to our minds unfold
One loving Soul throughout the universe,
Creates, directs, through ages yet untold,
Under fixed laws no vain desires reverse;
  Of His intent, enough we comprehend
  How finite, infinite, harmonious blend.

Should God in Christ His new Jerusalem
Build in this city, State, throughout this orb
Where men exist like rules must govern them,
And various needs their busy thoughts absorb;
Still higher motives may incite and spur,
Mould character, develop faculty,
With far more generous aspirations stir,
From all debasing shackles set them free.
   Mankind below in time that standard reach,
   His revelations souls degenerate teach.

For what we deem our destiny, reserved
For realms of spirit when our pilgrimage
Ends here below, however undeserved,
Our souls soar upward from this lowlier stage
To His companionship, and sacred host
Of great and good, who 've lived like us on earth;
If not all sinless, whom the Holy Ghost
Has made regenerate by the second birth;
   From care and sorrow here in course set free,
   We can conjecture what that life may be.

The steepled towers, that lift their graceful spires
Above the dwellings line our busy ways,
Denote the hope the soul devout inspires,
The creed that solace seeks in prayer and praise;

The more we scan the mysteries revealed
By what we learn of Nature or of mind,
The happier faith our sense and judgments yield,
Profounder truth that God is wise and kind;
Each man's experience forces to believe
The Gospel promises cannot deceive.

When Champlain first these tortuous paths ex-
plored,
When Winthrop here his thousand zealots brought,
To famished souls came ships with plenty stored,
The " Blessing of the Bay " the ocean sought.
Sedgwick and Leverett sailed from Frenchman's
clutch,
To snatch the meads and dales of Acadie;
Off from Manhattan Cromwell drove the Dutch;
From grasping Andros Bradstreet set us free;
No hostile fleet, no angry cannon's roar,
Dared havoc work within our guarded door.

From lofty Hoosac down to Cape Breton,
Here on the Charles, Phipps bore resistless sway,
And Plymouth Pilgrim and the Puritan
Alike King William's viceroy obey;
Thus strong, united, well might be defied

The hate of nations, jealousies of creed;
New England's sires extend their borders wide
With strife continuous and doughty deed.
  But Brunswick monarchs, heedless of the chance,
  At St. Germain gave Acadie to France.

The strife renewed, the gallant Pepperell
By Shirley sent, in secret left these gates,
His ships and army on the foemen fell,
And Louisburg surrendered in its straits.
France vexed, despatched an armament to deck
Our menaced city with its flaunting flag;
Our churches prayed for help; the fleet, a wreck,
Perished on treacherous shoal and beetling crag.
  When Wolfe, Montcalm, on Abraham's Heights
      were slain,
  From Pole to Gulf Britannia ruled the main.

Had Justice ruled her councils, not her pride,
With loyal colonies, her sway supreme
Had set at nought all the wide world beside,
Her brilliant promise proved no idle dream.
Americans of all too stern a stuff
To bow submissive to her haughty yoke;
France, her dominions lost, well pleased enough,
Gave help, which we reluctantly invoke.

And splendid fleets that here for succor came,
Their strength restored, the British Lion tame.

With France and England since in war arrayed,
Cruisers with hostile purpose hovering near,
Behind our shoals and strongholds, undismayed,
They boldly venture, come, and disappear.
Once the brave Lawrence, challenged forth to fight,
Went unprepared, and struck his flag to Broke;
Hull, Bainbridge, Stewart, all won laurels bright;
Perry, McDonough, the lake echoes woke;
   Yet, save for Freedom, Philip's War, or Shay's,
   No hostile shot within our borders strays.

Here first emerged upon her proud career
" Old Ironsides," in beauty clad and strength,
Whose brave exploits her memories endear
To our whole country, through its breadth and
       length;
Near Freedom's cradle generous Faneuil gave,
Whose patriot echoes reach from sea to sea,
Her keel was laid, till float upon the wave
She sailed in glory on to victory, —
   In breeze and battle, both in peace and war,
   Blest as the sacred chart whose name she bore.

Not far away from where she grew to life
Dock-yards lie idle, whence, in years to come,
Should glorious peace give way to mortal strife,
Cruisers as famous will the ocean roam,
Till learned the lesson by the blunders taught
Of other nations, millions spent in vain,
Builders whose vessels to perfection brought,
When needed, clustering on the seething main,
   Will shield our shores and fright away our foes:
   Such preparation better far than blows.

Still in all times whenever called to arms
To assert our rights, our country to defend,
Nowhere more glowing ardor stirs or warms,
More generous men their means and life expend.
Count the long list of patriots from the bay
That fought with Washington, for Freedom died;
Who dauntless flew to that fraternal fray
When the bold South our nation's flag defied;
   Mark on memorial walls our heroes lost,
   Their lives more precious than the conflict's cost.

If all were poor there would be none to give;
If all unlearned, no schoolmaster abroad;
The earth too small, if all were born should live;
With none to work, no bread upon the board;

Self-willed and proud, no thoughtful tenderness;
Each want supplied, invention must grow dull;
No home or family, no kind caress;
No pain or suffering, none be pitiful;
  For human kind, less suitable the world
  By social sages into chaos hurled.

In helpless infancy and wayward youth,
In manhood vigorous or decrepit age,
Obedience, honesty, and love of truth,
The various tasks our busy hours engage,
Place man in Nature's scale above the brute;
Build up his cities, wastes with plenty crown,
Give each his own, no idle tramps dispute;
Science, and art, and letters win renown
  As civilization, with its ceaseless tread,
  Goes marching on till round the planet spread.

CANTO XVI.

NOBLESSE OBLIGE.

THE crystal springs that from their fountains
    gush,
Dropped from the skies, drained through the earth
    below,
Drink from the stars, glow with the morning's flush,
Continue pure as into streams they grow.
If such the influences that nurse the child,
The lessons learned that shape his plastic growth,
His innocence by no base taint defiled,
Loyal and just, to all debasement loath,
    The child, unspotted in the honored man,
    Will carry out the Providential plan.

Such the conditions ever have prevailed
Since Puritan first made this shore his home;
Much that he added with success assailed,
For faiths may change as wiser we become.
All truths essential as the rocks must stand;
The wave may wash, the wintry tempest rend,
But while our country still is Christian land

No fallacies its firm convictions bend;
   Thousands of years our race may still progress,
   Till all shall practise what we now profess.

His life may harassed be, or rich, or poor,
His brightest aspirations turn to dust,
To honor, fame, or power, barred the door,
Be disappointed where most sure his trust;
Yet still, if just and true, his spirit brave
Accepts his fate, nor murmurs though forlorn,
Content to live, nor shudders at the grave,
Nor envies those to happier fortunes born;
   Bears both the good and ill with equal mind, —
   What nobler lot by God to man assigned?

It matters not how free may be the State,
Its laws how equal; privilege away,
Some will be bright, some rich, some good and
      great;
Wisdom will work, and sloth and dulness play.
Remove all bars that shut the alien out,
Extend the suffrage to the tramp and fool,
Pay the same wages to expert and lout,
Open alike to all the church and school, —
   Some men will roll in weath, while others crave
   The rags and crumbs the wealthy scorn to save.

Render that wealth unsafe, it taketh wings
To other lands more powerful to protect;
There shelter, food, and means to work with brings
Where worth and character command respect.
The harvest ripens once within the year, —
How without money, labor find its food?
The herds and flocks require time to rear,
The wingèd fowl but slowly raise their brood;
   Labor and capital not foes, but friends, —
   On this the welfare of them both depends.

Shame on the demagogues, for greed or place
Delude, cajole, and jealousies provoke!
Their objects gained but end in their disgrace, —
The world too wise to stoop to such a yoke.
Wealth may combine to multiply its yield,
Or toil co-operate for fair return;
Who shoot envenomed shafts against a shield
Will little glory in the medley earn.
   The mass of men, too sensible to risk
   The good that's theirs, will shun such basilisk.

In Rome of old the Catilines conspired,
Trampled on liberty to strut in pride,
By flattering lies the discontented fired,
Till to repress them, patriots allied,

Roused to its danger, the Republic saved.
At length the State, grown rotten at the core,
Its rulers base, its citizens depraved,
Plunged Italy in internecine gore;
  Tyrants in purple to the sceptre call,
  And Roman grandeur tottered to its fall.

And what delight would thrill our modern thrones
If like disaster overtook our land!
Yet here, as there, the peril: knaves and drones,
Cajoled and bribed, a worthless, servile band,
Too dull to see, vote as their leaders tell;
Trample on right and faith and equal laws,
For mess of pottage their prized birthright sell;
Who should its best friends be betray the cause
  By our heroic fathers bravely won —
  By their degenerate children now undone.

Is there no remedy?   Let nations stirred
By waste, dishonesty in high place, decide
Cure, reform, shall no longer be deferred, —
None serve the State that is not qualified;
Their public moneys shall no more be used,
Officials from their pay, to help, be held,
T' perpetuate authority abused;
The rats infest their treasuries expelled.

If none to vote till two score years and ten,
Their governments would vest in safer men.

Better for all the Scriptures to believe,
That man's great duty is to help and cheer,
Whatever chance with gratitude receive
To feed the hungry and to dry the tear.
Learning and wealth for others' good should toil,
Use, not abuse, the valued treasures lent;
From no hard effort, thankless task, recoil,
In carrying out their heaven-appointed stent;
   Knowing how swift our shadows speed their
      course,
   How soon the strongest will have spent their
      force.

Yield affluence its rights where justly true
To every loyalty it owes the poor;
Nor yet begrudge the honor justly due
Where God sees fit to give an ampler store;
Yet let no cringing soul the pregnant knee
In homage bend to selfish wealth, as wealth.
In nobler traits consists the high degree;
These claim respect, perhaps good sense and health,
   But not that worthless pride which in conceit
   Would all less favored tread beneath its feet.

In our broad land, by sacred Freedom blest,
If not all equal in our means and place,
No vain assumption should disturb the breast;
In life's long course the poor oft win the race.
In honor striving to increase our mite,
Prompt to relieve where others are in need,
In justice yielding every man his right,
And never faltering where its dictates lead, —
  We may be meanly clad and roughly shod,
  The "honest man's the noblest work of God."

Such the example generous Winthrop set,
When his last loaf to poorer neighbors sent;
And Haynes, and Vane, and austere Endicott
To those in want of their small surplus lent;
If Quaker Antinomian denied
Rest for the foot or shelter for the head,
The spacious earth was all too broad and wide
For restlessness in vain to crave for bread;
  This wilderness their own, they cared not share
  With dreamers, sought to plant a discord there.

Still they were Christians, and that term implies
Self-sacrifice and thoughtful tenderness,
Hearts all aglow with gentle charities,
Quick to relieve and solace all distress;

Though cruel laws, with fine and prison-cell,
Branded as crime to help the Quaker's need,
Their doors flew open, and their purse as well,
The ointment-box to stanch the feet that bleed;
   Preferred to brave the bigot's ruthless ire,
   Than drive the wanderer from their genial fire.

No need of laws to stimulate the heart
To yield to Heaven's behest obedience due;
If sorrow came, fit solace to impart,
To nurse the sick with tireless zeal they flew;
If famine, conflagration, spreading wide,
Reduced to penury or caused dismay,
What any had was lavishly applied
To soothe the pang or drive the care away.
   If dread calamity struck far from home,
   Even there their ready help was sure to come.

Here noble charities their records keep,
Whose welcome alms, bestowed for centuries past,
Since first kind souls their sacred coffers heap,
Nor less their loaves upon the waters cast.
The earliest relic of our ancient days,
Endowed by men from Scotia's rugged shores;
Another, at each Easter, feasts and prays,
Thousands made happy from its ample stores;

And many more, from loving spirits grown,
Their Christian faith by kindly act have shown.

Of all the ills to which frail flesh is heir,
What grief so poignant, or distress so dire,
That food or shelter ask, or tender care,
And craves in vain, no sympathy inspire?
The lame and maimed, the deaf and dumb and blind,
Of age or childhood each infirmity,
But homes, asylums, hospitals may find,
Physician, nurse, whatever needed be;
    Culture and wealth unite with hand and heart
    To soothe the aching brow or sorrow's smart.

Amid the host that here without parade
Their liberal means with the impoverished share,
Are kindly souls whose virtues need no aid
To justify the saintly wreaths they bear.
Of worth like theirs, be silent, reverent, —
No earthly praise they seek, or bliss divine;
The pang relieved, their grateful souls content,
The sacred charities their hearts refine.
    Within these walls the city reared they throng,
    To feed the hungry, make the feeble strong.

Its doors, in gracious welcome open spread,
Invite the poor to frankly state their need;

The soldiers maimed who for their country bled,
All that are destitute, to clothe and feed;
If helpless age or sore infirmity
Be left without support or near of kin,
Employment beg, to independent be,
Or counsel kind to save their souls from sin, —
  Our various charities together seek
  Work for the idle, bounty for the weak.

If anywhere within our border found
Those that need succor in their drear despair,
Skilled visitors, with each his special round,
With promptitude to learn the grief repair.
With painless touch they probe each aching soul;
Experience tells what best the pang t' allay;
If rooted vice their wretched lives control,
Their words of wisdom drive such fiends away;
  If food or fuel or the tenderest care,
  Whatever needed, — the want finds them there.

CANTO XVII.

CONCLUSION.

COULD human sense as the divine, supreme,
  Embrace in one clear view the course of time,
All that has chanced would be but troubled dream,
Too multifarious for this simple rhyme.
The dusky savage hunting here before,
The lonely Blaxton training fruit and flower,
The frolic maid, the first that leaped ashore,
Disease and death that in the future lower, —
  What prayers devout from their rude walls of clay,
  From saddened hearts to heaven winged their way.

Starvation menacing the wife and child,
The winter's cold that pierced their dwellings frail,
The prowling hordes, and beasts in forest wild,
Imagined foes in every hovering sail,
The selfish greed among themselves for place,
The good wives gathered to cast off their thrall,
Men scouting law that they might sin by grace,
A despot king that would his grants recall,

Ingratitude, as fostered viper, stung, —
Such the sharp thorns their sainted bosoms wrung.

Their wise delay their precious charter saved;
Their courteous acts the Frenchmen kept aloof;
Their lives austere discouraged the depraved;
Stocks by the Church administered reproof;
Strangers that chose such righteous rule dispute,
From lack of means or skill, a charge become,
Heedless to plant, and yet would share the fruit,
They warned away to seek some other home;
    Quakers were scourged, or dangled from the trees,
    Martyrs exhaled to sanctify the breeze.

The Indian chiefs perceive this ruthless ire;
With brand and rifle, to escape like fate,
By massacres and conflagrations dire
Sought to avert before it proved too late.
In vain they strive, in vain with blood they drench
Their native land, to keep what was their own;
Their council fires these useless slaughters quench,
Their country lost, their heroes they bemoan;
    And yet not long ere at the festive board
    The calumet relit, and peace restored.

The Stuart monarchs, tyrants to the core,
Brooked no resistance to their selfish sway;

Their minion judges trampled on the law,
By vile chicane our charter witched away;
Nor this alone, but like nefarious deed
Outraged the people, shook the tottering throne;
Charles' frighted soul beholds his father bleed,
James fled in terror lest that fate his own.
 Well might our stream that bore that father's
  name,
 For such a god-sire blush with kindred shame.

It had good cause besides; for Mather here,
Fond to believe that witches stalked the land,
Helped to create a foolish craven fear,
A strange delusion none could understand.
And simple souls with groundless terror wrung,
By sprites possessed beheld unearthly sight;
Scores were imprisoned, tortured, or were hung;
Many, suspected, perished in their fright, —
 Victims of phantoms that disturbed the brain
 Of priests and judges, of their wisdom vain.

Narrow, contentious, bigots, zealots, fought
Each for his creed, for others — cell or stake;
From such warfare, Christians refuge sought,
For these deserted shores their homes forsake.
Grim pestilence, with foul destruction dire

Stalking along the coast, had swept away
The Indian braves, and quenched their council fire,
The remnant all too weak such inroad stay,
 As saint and sage across the ocean flock
 To Strawberry Bank, or leap on Plymouth Rock.

Not to encroach on ground the Pilgrims plant,
On Mason's twenty leagues that inland swept,
The Plymouth council limit Winthrop's grant
Three miles below where Charles in trickles crept;
As many north of where the Merrimack
In larger stream from mountain gorges grown.
Not covetous, our sires for peace gave back
Vast areas were rightfully their own,
 Bounding far off upon the distant sea —
 Nor cared how far removed that sea might be.

Beneath yon marble, Bellingham lies dead;
Dummer, who bold the arms of France defied;
The generous Hancock, our first Congress led;
Adams, the claims of regal rule denied;
Sumner, whose brows judicial honors crown;
Sullivan, devoted to the infant State;
Gore's noble traits, more precious than renown;
Eustis, the loved physician as good as great, —

They need no monument; our annals tell
How well deserved the power they used so well.

Here Franklin's parents sleep in stately rest;
Faneuil, whose hall still cradles liberty;
Revere, to saddle sprang at Freedom's quest;
Paine, on the illustrious scroll, declared us free;
Cushing, denounced as eager for a throne;
Lothrop and Thacher; and a noble host
Famous throughout the world, or died unknown,
Their country's glory, or their city's boast,—
   Still echo through the years the homage paid
   When with due praise their coffins here were laid.

Still well remembered, what majestic shade
The Paddock elms cast on this sacred shrine,
Drawing their vigor from the havoc made
By Time's relentless tooth of forms divine;
Earnest the prayer that woodman spare these trees
That lent their beauty to the crowded street;
But traffic, all too difficult to please,
Trampled such idle thoughts beneath its feet, —
   Those noble trunks with graceful branches spread
   No longer sing the requiem of the dead.

Yet still within, above this sacred dust
Luxuriant growths wave on the perfumed air;

Stones may grow gray with moss, and plates may
    rust,
But records tell who have been buried there;
Thanks to the thoughtful souls who sowed the
    seed,
Belknap and Paine, who watered, trained, and
    pruned,
The memory kept of every word and deed,
To noble sires their living race attuned;
  Still throngs behold where laid, as passing on,
  Our earliest Mayor and his gifted son.

Phillips, peerless on the rostrum, battling for the
    right,
Whom no clamor daunted, no consequences
    swayed;
His lance in rest defiant, like some ancient knight
He charged whoever differed, with keenest point
    or blade;
Majestic as a viking, with sturdy arm and breast,
Nor minded whom he mangled, could he but strike
    the blow;
His weapons words that flashing, in choicest
    phrases drest,
Rolled on a mountain torrent, shattering in their
    flow, —

If not all believing his laurels worth their cost,
We admired him while living, are mourning him
   now lost.

In the dusky twilight closed that winter's day
When by this hallowed spot the mourners group,
And homage to their honored leader pay,
Their sad drums muffled, and their colors droop;
As the soft dirge comes floating on the air,
Within yon stately pile we stand agaze,
Views of his worth and genius we compare, —
Something to censure, yet with much to praise;
   If Heaven appointed to set free the slave,
   All must admit him eloquent and brave.

Who yearn for Nature have not far to seek,
Near every door the magic rug flits by;
When worn with care, our soul or body weak,
A wreath of parks with shade and sheen lies nigh;
There fountains gush, lakes wrapped in hills spread
     out,
Birds of red plumage tell their tales of love,
The lovers whisper and the urchins shout,
Beneath the cloudless vault of Heaven above;
   What matters it, if here be room for all,
   How many millions hers the city call?

Here Wampas roamed and ruled, and trapped his
      game,
His mother, the squaw sachem, dwelling near;
Tempting with gold the greedy white man came,
And one by one his forests disappear;
Till on our malls, by crafty men beguiled,
Where now the densest throngs surge to and fro,
He mourns in vain his native woodlands wild,
Then roves a sea-king where the tempests blow, —
    Till from his cell, for honest debts incurred
    The Merry Monarch freed the imprisoned bird.

Nor yet content, wrote knightly Leverett,
Wampas should have his lands, or payment made
For meadows, woods, from midst whose valleys wet
The infant Charles in winding courses strayed.
Was justice done? Ask pious Bellingham,
Whose ill-starred sister wooed the forest sprites,
As our first sorceress, came to special shame,
Off from her broom-stick on the scaffold lights;
    The river fountains still the story tell
    As they run murmuring down the weeping dell.

Yon dreary pile of solid, graceless stone,
What tales of woe its gloomy halls might tell!
Since Themis first could claim it as her own,

Her eyeless sword on none but miscreants fell;
There greed compelled to render up its prey,
The secret sin there often brought to shame,
Hope saw her fondest promise melt away,
And pride elate, all blurred its spotless name.
  . Happy the pure in heart its threshold cross,
    All undismayed, whatever be the loss.

Its honest bench in spotless ermine clad,
There earnest eloquence for justice pleads,
Defends the innocent, rebukes the bad,
Upholds the right, and all that's fair concedes;
Surely no abler men, or more upright
Than its forensic chieftains of the robe;
Whatever tempts them, keep their honor bright
As those, not mine to name, around the globe, —
    Jurists whose glory makes no idle vaunt,
    Unswerved by praise or favor, fear or taunt.

THE END.

www.ingramcontent.com/pod-product-compliance
Lightning Source LLC
Chambersburg PA
CBHW031110020726
47495CB00007B/2132